---- ★ ----

THE PLOT THICKENS

Detective Scott's gaze swept across the gathering of authors and would-be authors before he made his announcement. "You are all, collectively, under suspicion in the death of Muriel Lake, at least until the medical examiner releases the cause of death. Are there any questions?"

A hand was raised, and Gilda Shapiro stood up. "Where's Jonathan Pells?" she asked.

"And where's Alice Ludlow?" Cecilia shouted.

And then, as if on cue, the ballroom's double doors opened and Jonathan Pells and Alice Ludlow appeared, his hand on her shoulder.

The room erupted in pandemonium. The word *murderer* slithered through the room. And then the second accusation whipped behind it: *mistress...murderer...mistress...murderer...*

---- ★ ----

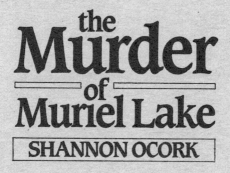

the Murder of Muriel Lake

SHANNON OCORK

WORLDWIDE ®

TORONTO · NEW YORK · LONDON · PARIS
AMSTERDAM · STOCKHOLM · HAMBURG
ATHENS · MILAN · TOKYO · SYDNEY

THE MURDER OF MURIEL LAKE

A Worldwide Mystery/May 1990

ISBN 0-373-26047-4

To the memory of the *real* Muriel Lake
I miss her

ONE

THERE IS A MOMENT in old ballrooms, before they wake again, when the ghosts come out and dance. If you are quiet and do not frighten, sometimes you can sense them.

Eduardo Vinici, banquet manager of New York's famous Hepplewhite Hotel, midtown at Fifth Avenue and Fifty-fifth Street, often felt the spirits in his party rooms in that dark instant when everything was ready but nothing had begun; from their mood he could predict an affair's success. An uneasy sleeper, he liked to rise on such occasions in the quiet predawn and take the elevator down from his attic suite to whichever room, all ready, waited. There, without turning on a light, he would pace from one end to the other and touch various pieces at random. And then he would sit where he could, have a cigarette and let the ghosts cavort.

Once the cigarette was done, Eduardo Vinici would lock the doors and go. If his left hand held steady, all would be well. But if it began to shake, he knew that he was being warned. Over the years he had learned how to hide this palsy; Mr. V simply slipped one hand inside his jacket pocket. At any rate, once the event was under way, the trembling stopped. And although some celebrations were happier than others, he had never suffered a real disaster. In his twenty-nine-year career—nineteen as banquet head—there had never been a fire, a major theft or a serious injury.

The possibility of murder he had never dreamed of . . . until now.

It is just those people, he told himself as, a little past four in the morning, he swung out of bed. *It's this new booking—these "crime buffs" who've got me going.*

An organization of authors, the Writers of Mystery, were about to open a four-day convention at the Hepplewhite. At 6:30 that evening the welcoming party began. The whole affair was to be relatively simple, more modest than most of the ones the Hepplewhite mounted. But almost from the day, six months ago, that Eduardo Vinici had first learned of the organization's plans, the specter of murder had invaded his sleep. He was tired to death of it. So he got up to consult the ballroom; to lay, if he could, the ghosts to rest.

Knowing that he wouldn't be going back to bed until the end of the day, Mr. V dressed properly: gray suit, yellow shirt, gray polka-dot tie, a fresh jonquil bud in his lapel. He brushed his graying hair with two different brushes and noted with satisfaction that his left hand was steady. Wristwatch, packet of mints, dark gray handkerchief in breast pocket, ring of hotel keys, two flick-point ballpoint pens inscribed with the Hepplewhite name, gold cigarette case, gold lighter, small notepad—he was ready. Before he left his suite, he made his bed and buffed the toes of his black Italian shoes.

The service elevator, decorated with brass and heavily polished wood, awaited him at the end of the quiet attic hall. When he pushed the old-fashioned manual crank, the door protested, then gave way with a creak. He made a note to have the runners oiled. Already there was a faint tingle in the fingers of his left hand; he willed it away. And then he caught himself checking the elevator—for bodies?—before stepping in. Mr. V grunted, closed the door and stood a moment, breathing heavily. Then he caught his reflection in the ceiling-mounted mirror and was comforted by the sight of his own, familiar face. Despite his inner unease, no fear showed. He smoothed his hair with his right hand and then pushed the button stamped 3.

The week Eduardo Vinici had been promoted to his current position at the Hepplewhite, there had been a murder in the hotel. A discharged cashier came back, confronted the personnel manager and shot the man where he stood. The cashier then gave himself up, crying, "That's the last time he'll ever fire anybody!" This statement was, of course, true, but as justification for violence it failed to satisfy. The ex-cashier was taken away in handcuffs and leg chains, the body of the dead man was removed and the incident was quickly forgotten. Even at the time no one had seemed to care. The press ran two paragraphs, no picture; one mention, that was all.

The elevator came to a stop and Eduardo Vinici stepped into a quiet corridor. Try as he might, he couldn't recall either the man's face or his name.

The corridor was empty.

He paused before the double doors of Ballroom A. Yes, he had definitely heard a noise. Somewhere. A foot slipping on a marble stair? The exit door to his left quietly closing? He put an eye against the crack between the doors and realized there was a light on in the room. He'd been told of a new man in room service who was supposed to be rather fresh with the kitchen girls. Perhaps the fellow was using the ballroom for one of his seductions. Well, he'd soon put an end to that, he thought, and to the young man, too.

His hand closed around the key ring; by habit his fingers distinguished the old-fashioned key. For a moment he wondered if he should summon a security guard before he entered, then sneered at his cowardice and, on a hunch, tried the knob of the right-hand door. Locked. Whoever was in the room knew he was trespassing.

Roused, the banquet manager inserted his key. Soundlessly the door opened.

Mr. V saw nothing untoward at first. The ballroom had been transformed, at the Writers of Mystery's request, into an English gentleman's library. Its rectangular contours had been carved into a gracious oval by set-in-place, eight-foot-high bookcases that curved away, flowed around and came back to the great fireplace in the west wall that looked down upon Fifth

Avenue. Giant Oriental rugs stretched over highly polished wood. Tall greenery stood in oversized copper pots. Long reading tables had club chairs pulled invitingly around them. The old grandfather clock that normally stood in isolated splendor on the landing of the main lobby staircase had been moved to the middle of the ballroom's shorter south wall. The clock lent a definite literary ambience, Eduardo Vinici thought; he had set it to sound the twelfth hour twice daily to add a mysterious air. It had been his own idea; his happy little surprise for the mystery writers. Mr. V paused to silently congratulate himself on another job well done, and then he saw the woman.

Muriel Lake, bestselling novelist of the penny dreadful kind. Committee head of the Writers of Mystery's convention. Relentless badgerer of Mr. V. She was down on her knees across the room among a pile of books, and in her lap was a large baby-blue box.

"My dear!" he exclaimed, extremely annoyed, "whatever are you doing here at this hour?" He hurried to her, smiling, one of his most professional smiles.

She was an attractive older woman, petite, well kept. Even this early she was smartly dressed in soft-skirted black silk, with red earrings that matched the enamel buttons on the bodice of her dress. Her golden page boy coif was tied back with a red ribbon.

She set aside the box at the sound of the banquet manager's voice. "Oh, Mr. V," she began, "I decided to come in tonight instead of tomorrow. I called and they said my room was available. Then when I got here I couldn't sleep. So since you'd given me a ballroom key, I thought I'd just make sure all the attendees' books were in proper alphabetical order. Remember I insisted on that? It saves face. It means no one's in the limelight." She was trembling, she who before had always been so controlled and so controlling. And she was very pale.

"The books are out of order?" he questioned, trying to keep his irritation from showing. Mr. V knew they'd been in perfect order. Muriel Lake had been a terrible bother through all the planning stages of the convention. Women. Say what you want, they weren't what they used to be. In fact, he wouldn't be surprised at all if Madame Lake's husband was the drunk he was rumored to be.

Muriel Lake gestured to the pulled-out books around her. "Just a few," she said. "I'll only be another minute."

Eduardo Vinici got down on his knees to help her. "Why, these are all yours," he said. And just then, reaching out to pick up *The Blonde Was All in Red*, his left hand began to shake uncontrollably. He clutched the book to hide the infirmity, then stood to find the book's place. The Muriel Lake mysteries were on the top shelf. At six foot one, he was able to reach up and insert it. "You're too short for this work, Madame Lake," he said.

"Miss Lake," she corrected him. "Or Mrs. Pells. My husband will hate it if you call him Mr. Lake."

Beyond her eyes, Eduardo Vinici pulled a face. Then, suavely, he said, "Why don't you hand the books to me in the order you want? I'll set them in."

"All right," she said, uncharacteristically agreeable.

They finished in a few quiet minutes. He took each book as she handed it up with his right hand and put it in line with his shaky left. She stood up with the last one, *Desperate*, her current bestseller. "I'll say good-night now," she said. She had the blue box in the crook of her arm.

Had she been weeping before he burst in on her? he wondered. There were smudges under her eyes and the stain on her lips was blurred, too. "Good night, my dear," he said, suddenly tender. "And don't worry. It will be a lovely affair."

"That's what all the men tell me," she said, "at the beginning." And then she smiled as though she'd made a little joke.

He watched her leave with relief. Five foot one or two, a size four, made for Adolpho suits and tight French dresses. Attractive, successful. Also selfish, domineering and rude: Hitler in a skirt. It was Eduardo Vinici's private opinion that there had to be something decidedly wrong with anyone who made a living out of murder.

The ballroom door closed behind her. Mr. V turned off the lamp. Then he sat before a window, lit a cigarette and waited for the dawn to brighten into day. The ghosts didn't have to dance in the dark room now to tell him that the week would be difficult.

His shaky left hand already had.

TWO

THAT NIGHT Cecilia Burnett sat down at her hotel room desk to begin writing in her diary.

It has been the most astonishing day, she wrote. The conference has begun at last and I'm part of it! As the newly appointed recording secretary of Writers of Mystery, known to members as WOM—the bat is our symbol—I'm to record all events.

This means I'll have entry to wherever I want to go and that I'll be able to introduce myself to all the people I admire. In fact, I met Muriel Lake today, twice, and can almost say that she and I are now friends. The second time she was arguing with her husband, fellow mystery writer Jonathan Pells, just outside the dining room before dinner. I almost bumped into them and they were really going at it. But, oh, I must be tired because I'm getting ahead of my story and a mystery writer cannot afford to do that.

Check-in began at noon. I was up half the night packing and repacking and fretting about my image. I don't mind being plain. I think that helps a woman writer in the beginning. It's my clothes. They simply have no style. Rexxy Oliver, my editor, says I must project a "literary image." You know, Mark Twain wore only white suits, Emily Dickinson liked lace collars. Think Bloomsbury, Rexxy said. Think Virginia Woolf. Oh, diary, can you imagine me, a person who looks like a cute Shetland pony—on a good day— creating the aura of Virginia Woolf? So I fussed and mussed the night away, rolled up my hair all crooked and then was afraid I'd oversleep. I set both alarms, five minutes apart, and lay down on the bed on the little patch that wasn't covered by rejected clothing, then slept as though I were dead. I dreamed that I was hiding in an outhouse. Bodies hung on hooks like bathrobes. And *they* were after me, with sharpened knives—whoever *they* were.

The alarms went off, but I slept through until nine and then woke up thinking I'd missed everything. So I just closed up my suitcase with whatever was in it, yanked the curlers out of my hair and leaped into my gray-and-green plaid suit that actually does show off my red hair and green eyes and fades my freckles a little. Then I shoved my feet into my loafers and I was off, and—yo-ho—early.

They let me check in, but I had to wait until noon for my room and a key that turned out to be a magnetic card. So I treated myself to breakfast in the Day Lily—all the Hepplewhite restaurants are named for flowers—and looked around to see what I could see. Or whom. But none of the early birds looked like writers, at least not until I spotted Muriel Lake as I was paying the bill. Hesitantly I approached her and introduced myself.

"Sit down and join me," she said, which was awfully nice of her, so I did. She ordered cinnamon toast and tea and asked me about my publishing career which, as you know, dear diary, isn't much at this point. But I told her about last year's *Death Takes a Slide* and my new novel, *Death Wakes Up*, which won't be out for another ten months.

Obviously she hadn't heard of me, which I understand. *Slide* wasn't last year's hottest book. But she was kind. She reminded me to look for my oeuvre, as she called it, in the library WOM had created in the ballroom. She asked who published me. When I told her Tombstone Books she seemed pleased. At least she said, "Congratulations, darling, you're with the best," and squeezed my hand. Muriel Lake is with Haunting House Press. Her *Desperate* has been on the bestseller list for at least a month, number seven or eight.

She had three copies of *Desperate* with her, and she autographed and gave me one. Thrill. She advised me to carry a copy or two of my own book around when I was out in public. "You never know who might be looking for a book to buy," she said, "and if they think that you just bought the one you're carrying, they might decide to buy it, too." Oh, we had a fine talk. But then this well-dressed couple walked in and the oddest thing happened. Muriel Lake paled at their sight, quite literally, and murmured, "Oh, no, please no!" She just bled white and froze with a piece of cinnamon toast halfway to the butter plate. The cou-

ple came over to our booth and Muriel introduced me
to Gordon Gates, the publisher of Haunting House
Press, and Alice Ludlow, who is *the* hot editor of the
year and, of course, Muriel's. They say that having
Alice as your editor is a better line of credit than a gold
charge card. They sat down, but before our conversation could begin I was paged—my presence was requested at the registration desk—so that was that.

I stood right beside Stanislas Yarrow, the espio-
nage writer, while I waited for my key. He's very
handsome and he, too, was beautifully dressed, wearing a light gray suit and carrying an expensive English
trench coat over his arm. I told him I'd read all his
oeuvre, and he winked at me. Another thrill. Then
Deirdre Day Tully—yes, *the* Deirdre Day Tully who
wrote *The Werewolf's Wife* and *Damsel in Distress*—
came up and took Mr. Yarrow away. She's elderly now
but imposing. She wears only black, like a witch: old-
fashioned black hightop shoes, black shawl over an-
kle-length black dress, brrrr. Most unusual, but I see
what Rexxy means; all these successful authors do
seem to have a definite image, each his or her own.
Well, after that I just came up here to my room, 444,
which looks out on a ventilation chute and is directly
over the ballroom, and flopped. I slept another hour,
then unpacked, showered and dressed for the cocktail
party, and the official welcoming at six.

I thought I'd go in right on time, not really knowing anyone and hoping that a smaller crowd would be
less intimidating. I'm glad I did because the whole

evening was a whirl. Writers are like overgrown children. They keep their creative channels open and that gives them a dangerous quality. Or at the very least a mischievous one.

Almost a hundred writers were already in the ballroom and the ones who weren't packed around the bar that was set up in the middle of the room at an old library table were searching the great wraparound bookcases for their oeuvre. On the scattered tables there were little reading lights and bowls of cut flowers. There was even an antique grandfather clock at the south end of the room. But the bookcases that surrounded the great room were what everyone was talking about. We all liked the effect.

One large man was complaining to another as I entered the room. The first snagged me and said, "You're the new recording secretary, aren't you? Last year I had that job and it's thankless, let me tell you." He told me his name, but I've forgotten now, after all the events that followed. The second gentleman of generous waist was WOM's paid secretary. He was the one, he said, who called me after I joined and asked if I'd take on the volunteer job. His name is Herman Patrick, but he writes under the name of Hermione Trick. He writes "women's suspensers," he explained, and so uses a woman's name. I said I would like to write a private eye mystery one day and that if I did, instead of Cecilia Burnett I'd use C. C. Burn. Both men said that would fly, and Herman/Hermione helped me fight through to the bar to order a drink.

I had my drink ticket ready and asked for soda water with lime. When I got it, Herman was gone and I didn't speak to him again the whole night. But I met two women authors who work together as a team. Their real names are JoAnn Morris and Gilda Shapiro and they write as JoAnn M. S. Gold. They do the popular Racy Lacy series. Both were brunettes, maybe in their fifties but chic, and they looked like sisters, especially because both were wearing the same dress. Gilda claims she wears two sizes larger, although I would have thought three. They pointed out Jonathan Pells, Muriel Lake's husband, to me.

Mr. Pells was standing by the gas-lighted fireplace drinking from a brandy snifter. He is a handsome man with a country gentleman look, all tweed and corduroy, with a shock of loose brown hair falling over his forehead. He was talking with our guest speaker for the evening, Sergeant Tyrone Scott, who is a working police detective and a neighbor of the Pellses. Muriel Lake bought an old millionaire's estate last year in Riverdale, which is a privileged little enclave in upper Manhattan along the Hudson River, and "Scotty," as everyone calls the detective, lives next door. "So I guess some policepersons make okay money," Gilda said. JoAnn thought that maybe he'd inherited it. I said maybe his house was the caretaker's cottage of the old estate, and both of them said that was a thought.

But then we were distracted because Muriel Lake, who is the committee head of our conference and the bright star of WOM—this year's darling, Gilda said—made her entrance. Muriel wore shimmering green taffeta and maybe even emeralds, too, and she was on the arm of her publisher, Gordon Gates. Alice Ludlow walked behind them; it was like a little parade, almost, or the arrival of royalty without the trumpets. Every eye in the room was on her, even her husband's, because I took a peep at him. The thought occurred to me that it must be hard for Mr. Pells, who was a good, although hardly successful, writer before he married Muriel, to watch his wife surpass him. Gilda whispered to me that Jonathan was a hard drinker who tried to keep off the "sauce" but sometimes failed. From the look of things tonight he was failing miserably. I saw him go to the bar three times for refills, and each one was a double.

And then came the shock, right before we were to leave the ballroom for the dining room next door. A bartender had turned off the reading lights with a dimmer switch to signal that they were no longer serving. That threw the long, oval ballroom into deep shadow. There was still a glow from the gas logs in the fireplace, and a lovely twilight came through the two gauze-draped windows that overlooked Fifth Avenue. Two waiters quickly pushed back the double doors at the north end of the room and a great ball of rosy light seemed to reach out to welcome us as the doors disappeared into their wall slots. I thought it a delicious moment, and in my mind congratulated whoever had set up these "special effects" for us.

I put my glass and wet napkin on the nearest table, preparing to move forward with the crowd. But then Muriel Lake stepped in front of the glowing pathway into dinner and asked for our attention. A shiver ran up my back. What a wonderful introduction I'm having into the world of mystery writers, I thought; I just love it and them to death.

"Darlings, I have an announcement to make," Muriel Lake said. She looked like an angel from heaven, brilliantly lighted as she was from behind, and all of us in dimness. I held my breath, not knowing what to expect but thinking maybe there would be a mystery to solve during dinner. Or perhaps there would be a coin in one of the dinner rolls and whoever found it would win a prize. But what our leader said was much different and much more serious. I couldn't take it in at first; it seemed so inappropriate to the fun we were having.

"I must tell you now so the rumors don't start," she began.

We all listened, as quiet as dust, except for Deirdre Day Tully, who sang out a single-high-pitched "ha!"

"My husband, Jonathan, and I have decided to divorce," Ms Lake said. "We remain the best of friends, our severing is amicable. It's very sad for both of us, but we're still the nice people we were before and neither of us is to blame. It's just one of the things that happens to a couple sometimes, and we would appreciate it very much if you didn't talk about it among yourselves." And then she turned with a swish of her taffeta skirt, took her publisher Gordon Gates's arm and led the way in to dinner.

Well, you can imagine the buzz. I don't even know these people very well and I'd only met Muriel Lake this morning, but I was as dumbfounded as the rest. I stood looking down at the tips of my brown sandals, not knowing what to do. Yes, I wore the brown dress with the orange stripe again. I know it's not glamorous, but it's loose and comfortable, and okay, I'll do better tomorrow. Gilda Shapiro, who was beside me, looked for Jonathan Pells and said, "His face is like stone. He's catatonic, poor man. He's just standing there, swirling his brandy. Oh, he must be devastated."

And JoAnn Morris, Gilda's "other half," said, "To think she'd emasculate him in this way. God, women can be cruel."

"She said it was a mutual decision," I threw in, feeling someone should support Muriel's side. "Maybe," I said to my toe tops, "he's as happy about it as she is."

"Hardly," said Gilda. "He hasn't written a word since they were married and that's five years. He burned out, poor thing, just when the little nobody he married got hot. Men haven't been taught how to deal with that kind of thing. They're not used to their partner being bigger than they are. A woman knows, oh, yes, but men still have that little dose of reality to learn."

I looked over then toward the fireplace where Jonathan Pells had been. He was still there, standing with Muriel's Haunting House editor, Alice Ludlow. The ballroom was clearing and everyone was gossiping as they made their way into dinner.

Mr. Pells was "stony-faced," I suppose, but he had the same look on his face he'd had when the party began. Yes, he'd been drinking heavily, but I bet my rent-stabilized apartment he'd known Muriel Lake's announcement was coming. It was Alice Ludlow who caught my attention. She was looking up at Jonathan Pells as if she were hungry and he was dinner. *Adoration* is the word. I remember when my sister Kristin married Bob Redweld. Oh, she'd chased him for years; he was her only love. But the day they married she didn't look half as cat-ate-the-canary as Alice Ludlow did just then. Ms Ludlow is one of those truly New York women who just breathe chic. She must get her hair done every day and trimmed every week, and she must throw out all of her clothes at the end of each season and buy new. Her hair is a perfect dark brown bob, her hands are beautifully manicured and her makeup looks utterly natural—she's a dream. If I were five foot eight instead of five foot four, with a voluptuous build instead of being a wisp, I'd die to look like Alice Ludlow. And there she was, gazing with open love at Jonathan Pells, and he wasn't even noticing.

Instead, his eyes were counting the ripples in the brandy he was swirling.

That's when I thought I'd visit the washroom. So I excused myself from JoAnn and Gilda and exited through the large double doors. At the far end of the corridor, on the left, is the ladies' room that can also be entered from the dining room vestibule at that end. Right beside it is the gentlemen's. And that's where, upon leaving, I almost stepped between Muriel and Jonathan arguing. Everyone else was already seated, and I saw that if I didn't hurry, I'd lose my fruit cup because the waiters were beginning to circle with those great aluminum trays they use for clearing tables. So I guess I wasn't looking and I walked right into Jonathan Pells's outflung arm. He was saying, "Either you tell Gates or I will. It's not fair to him or to me."

And she was saying, over his words, "I'll do it my way, Jon. Just stay out of my way. I warn you."

Well. I backtracked fast and scurried away. Gilda had saved me a seat between her and a "fan." A fan is an aspiring writer, an associate member who hasn't yet published. His name was Kevin Wilder, and he told me he had just finished his first novel and was looking for a publisher. I told him my house was Tombstone Books; that Augustus Graves was the top man; and that my editor was Rexxy Oliver. Rexxy is very good, I said, but she may be leaving to become a media expert on Wall Street. Kevin said that I was the most beautiful woman at the conference, which made me mad because I hate to be lied to. Bright, I would give him. Nice, I will also admit to. But gorgeous, please spare me. I told him that, straight to his face. "Please spare me," I said, and he left me alone after that, but he didn't take it back.

Forget what was served. Veal, I think, which I don't eat on principle. Veal producers hold baby calves in pens so that they can't exercise their muscles and give them only milk to eat. Then the calves are slaughtered and the meat is very tender. I disapprove of such methods. I mentioned this to Gilda, but she was more interested in Deirdre Day Tully—or DDT as she was known to her fans—who was sitting across from us and holding court.

DDT was saying that Muriel Lake had gotten too big for her britches. "If anybody should be sitting at the dignitary's table, it should be me," she said. Gilda, JoAnn and I all agreed. "But Lady Lake," DDT said, "in her effort to dethrone me has relegated me to members-only status. Well, she's running the show. This time. But need I remind you that my *Werewolf's Wife* was a bestselling book when Muriel Lake was still wetting her diaper? I do not. I had to remind her, though. Miss Mealymouth just said she was sorry, there was no room after Stash Yarrow, tonight's speaker, Herman Patrick, Gordon Gates and Alice Ludlow. But, kiddies, if you'll look, you'll see there's an empty place setting just to Muriel's right, and an empty chair. Now I ask you."

We all looked, and there was, indeed, a vacant place at the head table between Muriel and Jonathan Pells.

"Oh, I know," JoAnn Morris, who was on Gilda's left, said. "That place is for Augustus Graves of Tombstone Books. I wonder where he is."

The fan nudged me with his elbow when JoAnn said that, but I pretended not to notice and said inanely to the company, "I hope he comes. He's my publisher and I've never met him." Everyone looked at me as though I'd said a wrong thing, so I hushed.

DDT said there was a "war" going on between Haunting House Press and Tombstone Books over the top-notch mystery writers. "Your Mr. Graves," she said, acknowledging me, "published Muriel Lake's first novel—"

"*In Dire Extremis*," the fan said, but we ignored him.

"And it didn't go. But he stayed with her for several more books, slowly building her following. Then she married Jonathan, wrote *The Blonde Was All in Red*, but sold it to Gordon Gates, who made it her first bestseller."

"That's when the fur started to fly," Gilda snickered. "JoAnn and I had our first big book that year with Gordon, too."

"Oh? And which was that, dear?" DDT asked, looking down her nose.

"*The Midnight Music of Gustav Barr*," Gilda and JoAnn said together. They laughed and touched shoulders.

"I remember that one," Kevin announced.

"Did you ever read *The Catsup Bottle*?" DDT asked, cocking her skull-like head at our unpublished dinner partner. "Before your time, of course, but that was my first, a sensation in its day."

"Yes, ma'am," Kevin said ingratiatingly. "You and H. P. Lovecraft were my first love affairs in the world of books. Boy, *The Catsup Bottle* scared me to death. I still can't touch the stuff."

"Sweet," Deirdre Day Tully answered, and touched her mouth with her napkin to removed a stain.

By that time dinner was over and the pickup waiters pushed us back and forth as they took away the plates and things. And then Muriel Lake got up to introduce our speaker, Detective Sergeant Tyrone Scott of the NYPD. Scotty, as she encouraged us all to call him, was last in the line at the dignitary's table. When he stood up to hearty applause and Muriel sat down, Jonathan Pells moved over into the empty chair beside his wife and said something to her that made her snap back.

"Oh, I'm going to enjoy this week," DDT said, noticing, and she rubbed her hands together like someone cold seeking warmth.

Detective Scott talked to us about the value of skilled observation, for both policepersons and mystery writers. "Civilian eyewitnesses are notoriously bad," he said, and then gave us some examples. I was keenly interested—anything to help write a better book, you know—but I couldn't concentrate on the detective's speech because Muriel Lake and Jonathan

Pells got into a spat, right there in the middle of the dignitary's table. It started when the waiters served dessert, which was ice cream bombe shaped like a bomb, covered in chocolate with a cherry stem fuse. Jonathan Pells immediately soaked his stem in brandy, lit it and made a fire. Muriel snuffed it out with water from a glass and ruined his dessert, I guess, because then he switched their bowls and wouldn't let her have hers back and, oh, dear diary, then she began to rail at him and we couldn't hear the detective.

DDT was delighted. "I couldn't enjoy it more," she said as she watched her rival make a spectacle of herself. Kevin and I were annoyed; we wanted to hear what Scotty had to say. JoAnn and Gilda didn't say a word. They were turned away from me toward Scotty and they didn't look around. They just stayed stiff-shouldered and correct. By the time we got our "bombs," we were too intimidated to make any jokes, so we ate them bite by deliberate bite. Kevin tried. He switched my bowl with his. But when I gave him a stern look he stopped the comedy routine and finished his without another word. And the coffee in the pot was cold, too, by the time it came our way.

Detective Scott had doggedly plowed through his speech, but no one was listening. The attention of the entire room of over two hundred writers and friends was directed on Mr. and Mrs. Pells. They were hissing at each other, really having a go at it, and finally things ended when both of them pushed back their chairs, threw down their napkins and exited the room.

"Oh, good, now they'll kill each other," DDT said, and she barked her single laugh.

Scotty waited while they stormed out, and then tried to save what he could by saying, "Meanwhile..." A few of us clapped to encourage him, but he could do little to recapture our interest. He did say, I remember, that the events leading up to a crime were supremely important and that these were the things witnesses forgot. "We remember things we're supposed to see," he said. "But things that happen before the crime transpires aren't underlined in real life, and so we pass them by." I thought I could use that to my advantage in writing mysteries.

So the first evening sort of sputtered to an undistinguished close, diary, and so am I. It's almost midnight and the day begins tomorrow with breakfast at eight.

Cecilia closed the leather folder she had been writing in, turned off the lamp and climbed into bed. When she closed her eyes, thoughts and images tumbled in her mind. And then she heard a clock strike a heavy, solemn, reverberating *bonnnggg*. It came out of the darkness, a strange and doom-impending *bonnnggg*, *bonnnggg*.

She lay there and tried to determine from what direction the repeating tolls were coming, but they seemed to ascend from everywhere. She counted the strikes: twelve times the mysterious clock chimed the hour. Midnight. She relaxed, thinking all was over.

And then...a resounding crash caused her whole room to shiver, and the glass in her bathroom rattled against tile.

She got up, mentally kicking herself for not packing a robe and slippers, and thought about putting on her raincoat and sandals and investigating. Still wearing her slip, she unchained and opened the door of her room, and peered up and down the corridor. Apparently, no one else had been disturbed; the hallway was empty. She waited, her heart pounding against the door edge. It's nothing, she thought, this must happen in hotels all the time.... But shouldn't a good mystery writer investigate? She remained leaning against the door, tired, not wanting to dress entirely, wondering what people would think if she were spotted traipsing around the hotel in a slip and raincoat.

Finally Cecilia closed her door and went to the telephone on the table beside her bed and dialed 3. The operator was quick to answer.

"I heard a crash," Cecilia said. "I'm in 444. Is there a party going on, or has there been an earthquake?"

"No, ma'am. All the private party rooms are closed now. Only the Gardenia Room, with its piano bar is open."

"If you're in the middle of a robbery, say 'wake-up call,'" Cecilia said.

"No, ma'am. Good night." The operator disconnected.

"It must be my imagination," Cecilia scolded herself. "The cleaning crews are moving furniture, that's all."

She climbed back into bed, her heart slowing in spite of her thoughts. And in the darkness she finally slept.

THREE

"YOU MUST COME immediately to the ballroom and take control," Eduardo Vinici yelled into the phone.

"Do I have time for a shower first?" Detective Sergeant Scott asked.

"No, please. Hurry."

"I'm on my way," Scotty said. He rolled out of bed and pulled on his clothes. He didn't lose time wondering what the excitement was all about. Long ago he had learned that he would know soon enough.

Mr. V opened the ballroom doors for him, from the inside with a key. Although the banquet manager now seemed calm, his left hand was shaking violently.

"Calm down, sir," Scotty said kindly. "Just show me what the trouble is."

"Dear God in heaven," said Mr. V, closing and locking the doors as soon as Scotty was in the room. "The southwest corner," he said faintly, as if afraid of being overheard.

Scotty looked. The curving bookcase was overturned and books lay scattered. As he moved toward the corner, the banquet manager flicked a switch that turned the table lamps to full strength.

Under the bookcase, under an avalanche of fallen books, lay Muriel Lake. She was facedown, virtually buried. One outstretched hand, clawed free of the wreckage, clutched a volume of *Desperate* in a death grip.

Scotty suppressed a cry and bent to her.

Golden hair was tangled dark with congealed blood. He touched her hand, knowing it would have a strange, cool stiffness. His stomach heaved. "Ah, no," he said, and looked up at the banquet manager quaking above him.

Mr. V crouched beside him. "I came in here at five," he said, "as I usually do, to open the room, to check. I locked it last night myself, just around eleven. The room had been cleaned and everything placed in order during dinner in Ballroom B. Everything was fine when I left." He steadied his shaking left hand on Scotty's shoulder. "At eleven last night," he said, "this hadn't happened. I'll swear to it."

"First," Scotty began, "tell the staff to bolt those sliding doors into the dining room and keep everybody out of here. Second, call your precinct. What's this, Midtown South?"

"I have the number," Mr. V said. But he stayed down beside the detective. "The publicity," he whispered.

"Third," Scotty continued, "have someone bring me a pot of coffee. A big pot and I use cream. Where are the writers having breakfast?"

"Next door. They use the same room for all meals. Breakfast's a buffet. They're setting it up now. The doors open at 7:45." The banquet manager stood then, and his knees cracked. "There's no way to keep them from knowing." His left hand shook in his jacket pocket.

"We'll make an announcement," Scotty said. "We'll ask them not to talk to the press until we've made our report. Forget asking them not to discuss it among themselves. That would be impossible."

"They're all writers," Mr. V agreed, trembling. "Every last one of them."

"Go now," Scotty ordered, "and then come back to me. Do you have other parties, other functions, going on now, too?"

"Florists," the banquet manager said. "Tonight and Wednesday. And several private luncheon parties this afternoon. I can contain them, in the main. Though what people talk about in elevators—well, there's little I can do. The afternoon papers will have it out on the streets by three, and then, oh, bless me, there'll be the TV. We can't turn off all the televisions in the hotel. We simply can't."

"Call the police and get me some coffee. Bring her husband, Jonathan Pells, when you come back. Do you know which room they're in?"

"The Franklin Delano Roosevelt Suite," Mr. V said, sighing. "Fourteenth floor, overlooking the avenue. Twin double beds, wet bar, terrace. Very nice." And then he was gone, and Sergeant Scott was alone with the body.

A new day's light filtered through the windows overlooking Fifth Avenue. Scott heard the awakening city, he heard the honking and screaming. "Oh, baby," he murmured, still crouched beside the body. He stroked a lock of gleaming golden hair. "Oh, Mu, this isn't the way any of us wanted it to end, is it?"

FOUR

ROMEO POPOI, recently transferred by hotel management from room service to bellman trainee because of his inability to concentrate upon his work while in the presence of female staff, knocked without success upon the door of the Franklin Delano Roosevelt Suite. Finally, using his master key, he let himself into the spacious foyer and stood uncertainly. A large vase of forsythia faced him. Around a curve of wall discarded male clothing littered the rose carpet.

"Mr. Pells? Mr. Pells!" he called. The unmistakable sound of snoring came from the direction of the open bedroom. "Mr. Pells, oh, please!"

Romeo was afraid to advance and reluctant to retreat. He wanted his job; he had been warned that if he didn't "straighten up his act" he wouldn't survive his probation period. He moved into the sitting room, located a telephone on the fancy walnut bar and dialed the operator.

"Will you please ring this room?" he requested. "This is Popoi, and I'm to bring Mr. Pells down to Mr. V, but I don't want to barge into the bedroom. He's sleeping soundly."

"Yes, of course," the operator responded impersonally.

Romeo didn't know her. He replaced the receiver and noticed a note scrawled in pencil on a hotel pad beside the telephone—"*Sin* in the library." He thought for a moment, then tore the page off and stuck it into a pocket of his trousers.

The telephone rang and he jumped. His hand moved toward the receiver, but he stopped himself in time. He waited for the snores to stop and for Jonathan Pells to answer. But the telephone continued to ring and the snores rolled on. Wake up, Romeo prayed silently. Don't you know your wife is dead? Wake up!

The telephone stopped ringing.

Romeo advanced to the bedroom door and banged his white-gloved fist upon it. "Mr. Pells, wake up, sir," he shouted. The curtains at the window were drawn. The room was very dark, but he could see that one of the two double beds hadn't been slept in. Two gold-foil-wrapped mints still rested upon a pillow, and the pale coverlet was untouched, its corner folded back in the Hepplewhite style. Romeo moved to the curtain cord and opened the draperies. Sunlight spilled into the room, but still Jonathan Pells didn't budge.

"Mr. Pells, sir, I must insist," Romeo said with courage. He advanced to the bed where the man lay submerged under pillow and blanket and shook what he hoped was a shoulder. "Mr. Pells, you must wake up."

Only deep and regular snoring answered.

Romeo was furious now. He attacked the shoulders of the sleeper and shook for all he was worth. "Mr. Pells, Mr. Pells!" Something stirred, and Romeo repeated the exercise.

The body in the bed twisted, and a whiskered face with its eyes closed appeared. "Darling, you called?"

"Mr. Pells, sir, you must get up. You wife is dead." In Romeo's frustration he had blurted out the very information he had been ordered to keep to himself.

"Not her," came the rumpled reply. "She's immortal, like carbon 14. Go away."

"Mr. Pells!"

The telephone rang again.

"You get it," Jonathan Pells said as he flopped over and pulled the pillow back over his head.

"This is an emergency!" Romeo screamed.

"Every morning is an emergency," Pells mumbled. "Call me in the afternoon."

The telephone stopped ringing.

Furious, frustrated, Romeo pulled the covers off Jonathan Pells and shook the man's shoulders again and again. "Your wife is dead, sir. Your wife is dead. Get up! Get up!"

"All right if it means that much to you." The writer rolled over onto his back, flipped the pillow behind his head and opened his eyes. "Bring me coffee, and a double tomato juice and a bottle of Worcestershire sauce, and make it snappy."

Romeo stood tall. "There's no time for that, sir. You're wanted in the ballroom by the police."

"Why?" Jonathan Pells asked.

"Your wife is dead!"

"Scotty'll handle that," Pells replied, scratching his jaw. "You handle breakfast. Now get out of here."

"Yes, sir," Romeo said, considering his mission done. "Just get up."

"I am up. Bring me breakfast and the *New York Times*."

"Sir, your wife is dead. A bookcase fell on her last night."

At that Jonathan Pells sat up and laughed.

The bellman backed away. No hope for a tip this time, he thought. No one rewards the bearer of bad news; his father, a former hotel man, had taught him that early on.

ONCE ALONE, Jonathan Pells rang Scotty's room. When the operator interrupted to ask if he would like to leave a message, Jonathan almost said no, but reconsidered. He gave his name, replaced the receiver and lay back for a moment against the bed's headboard.

I am not a good man, he thought. It hurt him to acknowledge that fact.

Muriel dead? Impossible. She was pulling another of her publicity stunts. She'd been planning this WOM convention for a year, figuring ways to get all she could from it. Muriel was only playing dead, gaining front-page notoriety to boost sales of *Desperate*. For the ruse to be effective, she had kept him in the dark.

But he bet that ass of a publisher Gordon Gates knew what the little darling was up to.

Agatha Christie had done something much like it on the publication of *The Murder of Roger Ackroyd*. And come to think of it, Ms Christie and her husband had been in the process of divorcing then, too. By damn, of course, that was it! That was exactly how Muriel's devious mind worked. She was copying Christie and she'd get reams of publicity out of it. He wished, fleetingly, that he was as cleverly manipulative as his wife. He would never be so—he was a contemplative man, unMachiavellian. And, yes, he could admit it to himself, he abhorred physical confrontation. But not Mu. She was a hundred pounds of bullet, always ready to fire. And Jonathan admired that.

Wait a minute.

Had wifey dearest set him up last night? Started a public argument to put him under suspicion? He wouldn't put it past her. All right, he'd fallen off the wagon, his fault entirely. But Muriel had been the cause of that, too. She'd reneged on her promise to tell Gordon Gates the truth, and he'd needed to get up the courage to face Gordon himself. Of course, he hadn't yet. That ridiculous announcement she'd made last night before dinner had stopped him; she'd said she'd stop him and she had. Ah, dolls. We should never have let them learn to read. See what they do with their education. . . .

Scotty.

They'd gotten into it over Scotty. Now he remembered. Scotty had *poked* her, she said; his wife and his best friend getting it on behind his back. He'd wanted to kill her then. For one tiny moment he'd really wanted to choke her. Funny, shouldn't it have been Scotty he'd been mad at?

Carefully Jonathan Pells eased himself out of bed. Naked, he practiced walking like a sober man to the bathroom, and then stood under a hot, needle-sharp shower and felt his anger surge all over again.

Scotty. Tyrone Scott, who'd said he understood what it was to love like crazy and then not feel anything anymore. Let her go, Jonny, Scotty had argued. You don't need Mu. You can make it on your own....

Someone was standing beside the shower stall.

Jonathan thought it was the bellman back with breakfast. He banged open the shower door, but as he was about to throw a bar of soap at the upstart, he realized it was Scotty, hands in his jacket pockets, face solemn and correct.

"Jonny," Scotty began, as though he hadn't betrayed him, as though they were still best friends. "Jonny, I'm so goddamn sorry. I loved her, too, you know."

Lathered with soap, streaming wet, Jonathan plunged out of the shower. His fist smashed against Scotty's cheekbone, and Scotty's head bounced off the bathroom tile and he went down. Jonathan stepped back into the shower and closed the door. He began singing "Dixie" at the top of his lungs.

"Stop singing, you son of a bitch," said Scotty from the floor. "Don't you understand? Muriel is dead."

FIVE

GORDON GATES SAT as far away from the buffet table and the writers as he could possibly get. He didn't want to be bothered by "little novelists" during his breakfast. Impatiently he waited for his editor, Alice Ludlow, to bring him his coffee, prune Danish and juice. Alice was a good editor and an attractive woman, but Gordon had never been in love with her. He thought that was because he had never trusted her. Alice kept so much hidden, so much repressed. If she had married, he thought, she might have become a wonderful woman, responsive, expressive, amusing. Like Muriel Lake. But Alice always kept her thighs together. That's how he thought of Alice Ludlow: grammatically correct and closed-thighed.

Muriel's death was nothing short of a disaster to him. No sooner had he found himself a novelist who could sell more than five thousand copies in hard-cover than she died under the weight of her own first editions. Incredible. It could mean the complete and total collapse of Haunting House Press. The European cartel, Tout Livres, had been trying to take him over for a year. And that thief Augustus Graves of Tombstone Books had already offered twice to buy

him out at a bargain-basement price; *everybody* knew
he was in trouble. He'd had to mortgage everything he
had after Haunting House lost a slander suit over a
book they'd published accusing the town of Emily of
being a breeding ground for spies and witches. And he
had counted on, *banked on*, Muriel's new book to pull
him out of the hole. *Desperate* was doing well, but he
needed the follow-up novel, *Unforgivable Sin*, before
he'd be even, much less back in the black. Muriel was
to have submitted the manuscript to Alice yesterday,
but she hadn't. "One more read-through, darlings,"
she'd said. "I'll give it to you at breakfast, I promise." Well, he'd get that manuscript before lunch, over
Muriel's dead body if he had to. Even if he had to talk
to Jonathan Pells who, irony of ironies, had written
the blasted exposé, *Evil in Emily*, which had brought
Haunting House Press to the brink of ruin.

Gordon Gates sat in his chair hating Jonathan Pells
and watching Alice make her precarious way toward
him, carrying far too many dishes. His glass of orange
juice tilted dangerously over the Danish dish. Just his
luck to have breakfast spoiled, too.

"It would suit my mood if you'd crash," he said as
she neared.

Concentrating, Alice said mildly, "Take the orange
juice glass off first, Gordon." He did, and she put
down the stacked coffee cups and a plate of assorted
pastries. Then she sat herself down, her back to the
room, and said, "Only for you and only under these
extraordinary circumstances would I humiliate my-

self like this." She pulled an empty plate from under the full one, served herself a croissant and busied herself cutting it into pieces. "I've got the whole story now," she said, "as much as is known. Already everyone is embroidering and embellishing things to fit his talents."

"The manuscript," Gordon Gates said, lowering his eyebrows as someone approached their table. "You get that manuscript, Alice, or you'll soon be waiting on tables for a living."

Alice Ludlow said nothing. She sipped black coffee. Alice wasn't worried about her career; she knew she could always go with Tombstone.

"Mr. Gates," a high-pitched, timid voice said, "my name is Herman Patrick and I write suspensers. I was at the dignitary's table with you last night. I'm executive secretary of WOM. May I sit down?"

Gordon said nothing.

"Table's free," Alice finally replied, and gestured invitingly.

"I've published fourteen paperback originals under the name of Hermione Trick," Herman Patrick began, nervously smoothing his shirt around his waistband as he sat in the empty chair between Gordon and Alice. "But I've got a great idea for a hardcover. I'm ready to break out."

"I've only a moment to spare," Gordon said. "This tragedy..." He bit deeply into his Danish, getting prune jam on his upper lip.

"Sir, I understand," Herman Patrick said, pulling his chair closer for confidentiality. "I can tell you in a word. Its working title is *Murdered*. The whole novel is told in the voice of the corpse while it's being buried. While the coffin is lying there in the ground with all the mourners around. The corpse can see because the soul is a free spirit and it can hear, but there's a twist. It doesn't know who the murderer is, so it has to listen to the comments of the suspects around the grave and then when it figures things out—"

"Send Alice three chapters and an outline," Gordon interrupted. "We'll take a look."

Herman Patrick, agile despite his bulk, leaped up from his chair. "Oh, thank you, Mr. Gates. I know you're going to love it."

Gordon didn't attempt a smile. "Now if you'll excuse us..."

"Sir, I'm gone," Herman Patrick breathed, and he stepped quickly away back to a table of cronies.

Respectful silence greeted the man when he sat down. Alice watched the writer lean into the table, stroking his beard with the smugness of a cat as he told his friends his good luck. They'll all come after Gordon now, she thought, and she smiled at how he would hate it.

"Herman's a nice man," she said. "And he's a diligent writer. Maybe with some hard editing, if his execution's good, we could do something with him."

"Alice, just bring me *Unforgivable Sin*. Deliver it safely into my hands. Then I'll buy all the junk you want. Find that beast Pells, romance him a little if you have to. Just bring the bacon home to daddy. I want that manuscript before lunch. Please.''

''You don't often say please, Gordon.''

''That's how desperate I am.''

Alice ate her third bite of croissant. ''Now let me tell you all I know about what happened to Muriel.''

''Tell,'' Gordon Gates encouraged. His Danish was gone, so he chose a fat cheese-and-almond croissant and sliced it in half with a vicious swipe of his table knife.

''At eleven last night,'' Alice began precisely, ''Mr. Vinici locked the ballroom after checking to make sure it was ready for today's functions. But Muriel had a spare key. The only spare key. Muriel and Jonathan went upstairs after their public spat. They continued fussing at each other till about 10:15 or so when Jonathan, according to Sergeant Scott, fell into bed, drunk. Muriel must have gone down to the ballroom, let herself in with her key and started to check her books in the bookcase. You know how short she is—''

''A sixty-two-inch stack of money was what Muriel was,'' Gordon Gates interjected, ''and, baby, that's tall.''

Alice Ludlow sighed. ''Physically short, then, Gordon. Muriel must have tried to climb up on the bookcase to reach one of her books—she had *Desperate* in her hand when she was discovered—and somehow she pulled the entire bookcase over on herself. It was one of the double-width, curving ones, very heavy, especially with all the books in it. Her head was crushed. What a terrible way to die.''

"Oh, not so bad," Gordon argued, feeling better as he watched the "little novelists" drift out of the room and away from him. "It was quick. Probably the edge of a shelf hit her in the right place and, bingo, death was instantaneous. We should be so lucky."

Alice kept her eyes down as she drank the last of her coffee. Sometimes she didn't understand Gordon Gates's mind. At other times she understood it only too well and disliked him the more for it. It wasn't that Gordon was a bad man, she thought. He was just hard and insensitive. Sometimes it was as if he wore blinkers. He lacked subtlety and thought gentleness should be reserved for special occasions. "The medical examiner who was going to address us tomorrow was called in," she continued. "He's now going to speak at dinner tonight. Whoever's taken over has rearranged things in a hurry. If I'm going to get Muriel's manuscript, I'd better start now. We're on the seminar that starts at ten."

"Go," Gordon agreed, and he sat back and lit his first cigarette of the day.

Alice collected her bag and briefcase. "You'll get cancer," she said. Gordon made a face. She'd hit home and she was glad. Yes, she thought, I can handle Gordon Gates and whatever he dishes out because more people will hire me than I'll ever work for, and because I know how to lead him to water and how to make him drink.

The water was Jonathan Pells and the drink was getting Gordon to publish him again. And that's what Alice Ludlow wanted—*desperately*.

SIX

SCOTTY WASN'T SURE. He was in the ballroom with Lieutenant MacNeil of Midtown South, Jonathan Pells and Dr. Fu Song, skeptically surveying the death scene. The body of Muriel Lake had been sealed in a body bag and moved to a gurney. Two paramedics stood beside it with folded hands, waiting the order to move. The fallen books still lay scattered on the floor, and a chalk line outlined where the body had lain. The bookcase had been set back into place, and Romeo Popoi was at work replacing the fallen books. Dr. Song had said he saw no reason to suspect foul play at the moment. It appeared that the victim had been unable to bring down the book or books she was after, had stood on the first shelf and reached up. Failing, she had grabbed the top shelf, lifted herself, and the now top-heavy bookcase had fallen on her, striking her in two fatal places: on the right temple and on the back of the head. The temple injury had been serious; the head injury had been fatal, caving in the skull. She had also been bruised by the falling volumes.

But Scotty wasn't sure.

He had a red welt on his cheek that would soon be purple, and his jaw was stiff from where Jonathan had belted him. His head ached from hitting the bathroom wall, but he wasn't in any way seriously injured. It took a lot to kill a person, he thought, even a five-foot-two-inch, hundred-pound person. It took malice and intention and boldness.... Yes, a person could be struck by a falling bookcase and suffer a concussion. But the odds that a falling bookcase would deliver such a clean, perfect hit were small. Possible, granted, but... And then there was the sinister humor of it all—the mystery writer beaten to death by all her books, as though they hadn't liked how she had written them and they had malevolently ganged up on her. It's too human this accident, too amusingly cruel....

"How would it be different," Scotty asked, unconsciously massaging his jaw where it hurt, "if she'd been purposely battered, struck, say, with a book?"

Dr. Song cocked his head. "Well," he said, "batterers usually don't use books, Detective Scott. Classically they use their fists or open hands. They shove and slap. They're frustrated bullies. They don't intend to injure the victim as much as to intimidate or punish. They always seem surprised when you accuse them of actually hurting anyone."

"But if one did?"

"Well." Dr. Song was a small man and almost girlishly pretty. Barely more than thirty, he was bright, ambitious and inexperienced. He had been with New York City's Medical Examiner's Office for only four months, his first job after completing his medical internship. "One of those books—" he gestured at the jumbled pile "—probably weighs about a pound. The bigger ones, maybe two. Most of them are light-weight, literally speaking. If the victim was hit with the front or back of the book and not the spine, the trauma of contact would be spread over a wider area. No, I don't think book battering's a possibility here."

Scotty was silent then, thinking.

Jonathan spoke, his first words since he'd made his statement to Lieutenant MacNeil. "A gavel," he said. "You could crack a person's skull with a gavel if you swung it hard enough."

"Perhaps a very heavy one," Dr. Song agreed politely, snapping his medical bag closed, "but I see no gavels here, Mr. Pells, and no evidence that Ms Lake was hit with intention. Oh, I can see how a group of mystery writers would think murder when it was only an accident, but I think you'll be disappointed. I will, of course, do an exhaustive autopsy, but unless I find actual evidence, I won't speculate or entertain fantasy. Murder, gentlemen, to me at least, is not a parlor game."

"Fair enough," Scotty said, staring at the upper right-hand corner of the bookcase. There were scrapes on it, and there had been blood. The corner had hit Muriel's head somehow when it had fallen. He couldn't dispute that.

"Whoever Muriel came into this room to meet killed her," Jonathan Pells said, without emotion.

"Her lover. One of her several lovers. Turned nasty from being betrayed."

"There's no evidence anyone was in this room last night beyond your wife," Dr. Song pointed out gently. "There was no conversation overheard that's been reported, no raised voices. There are no signs of physical disturbance other than the bookcase itself. Each little table light and vase of flowers remains in its place, sir, undisturbed. I'm sorry. I know you're distressed." The doctor turned and gestured to the paramedics. They stationed themselves at the gurney. "Until this evening, then," he said, bowing to Jonathan Pells. To Lieutenant MacNeil and Detective Scott he said, "I'll call you as soon as I know the results."

"Thanks," Lieutenant MacNeil said. "There's no case unless the doc here says there is, and it looks as if he won't," he said to Scotty. "But if there is a case, it's yours. You caught it."

"There's a case," Scotty said. "I can feel it."

"We'll see," MacNeil returned. "I'll work with you, give you all the help I can if that's how it turns out. Shame, huh? Pretty lady doing all right for herself, then, no reason, just gone. It happens that way sometimes."

Scotty shook the lieutenant's hand and let him go. Then he turned back to Jonathan, who was sitting in a club chair watching the bellman slowly replace the books in alphabetical order.

Scotty stood before Jonathan. "Okay, I shouldn't have done it. I admit that. Hell, I was halfway in love with her, you know, and you weren't anymore. But, okay, I'm sorry. I shouldn't have. It was only once and neither one of us felt good about it after. But at the time it seemed right. It was the night you accused her of stealing your work, remember? Maybe you don't. You were in the bag at the time. It was the night you crawled upstairs to go to bed. She told me living with you was killing her. I told her to leave. We used the sofa. I'll leave this hotel as soon as I can, but as it stands I've got to wait to hear from Dr. Song. Then, if he gives the word, I'm out of here and out of your life.''

"Herman Patrick has a gavel," Jonathan Pells said, looking at nothing. "Yesterday afternoon, in our suite, he showed it to Mu and me. Brand-new, he'd just bought it. He's going to initiate it at the meeting Thursday afternoon. It was heavy, square-edged and the ends were silver-plated.''

"Where is it now?''

"Last night when Muriel left she had it. Herman forgot it in our suite. She said she was going to his room to give it back to him. But then she always was a liar, wasn't she?''

"We're all liars," Scotty said. "Sometimes, some ways." He walked away.

Jonathan didn't seem to notice. But Romeo Popoi did. The bellman paused, a large dictionarylike black book in his hand, and watched the detective cross the room and let himself out. Then Romeo opened the book, which was actually a small safe. "Here's your murder weapon, Mr. Pells,'' Romeo said, holding the book out to Jonathan. "It must weigh forty pounds."

Jonathan didn't seem surprised. He got out of his chair, took the object from Romeo's hands, felt its weight and nodded. "On the flyleaf," Jonathan began without opening the cover, "there's a dedication: 'This book, and everything that's in it, I give to my darling wife. Kisses, too. JP.' I gave it to Muriel on Christmas Eve, two nights after she banged my best friend. At the time it held pearls."

Romeo Popoi wet his lips and smiled. "And now, sir?"

Jonathan looked. Now it held a book contract. And along the rim of the safe, where the upper spine protruded over gilded metal cut to resemble pages, were crumbs of blackened blood.

SEVEN

A MAID'S CART almost blocked the entrance to the Franklin Delano Roosevelt Suite, and because the door was ajar Alice Ludlow didn't knock but walked right in.

A voice with a Jamaican accent boomed from the bathroom. "I'm almost done, honey. You want me to leave and come back?"

"Oh, no," Alice said as though the well-appointed suite were her own. "Go right on. You're not bothering me." The sound of a tap turned on was her answer. She checked the bedroom for Jonathan, but he was obviously not there. Quickly she began to search, trying to think like the super-organized Muriel. There were a number of copies of *Desperate* on the dresser top, and Muriel's briefcase was tucked between the dresser end and a corner of the wall. Alice sat on the bed to glance inside the case, but all it contained were exhaustive notes on the WOM convention, including who was supposed to be where, what Muriel would be doing and with whom. Curious, Alice looked at Muriel's agenda for Monday night after dinner. There were only initials after that evening's dinner notes: AG. No time, no place.

Augustus Graves, interpreted Alice. Tombstone Books, our rival. Or Gordon Gates's and Haunting House Press's rival. Augustus Graves had once wooed Alice to leave Haunting House and join Tombstone; Alice had said no. Later he had offered to buy Gordon out after Haunting House lost *The Evil in Emily* suit and the book had ended Jonathan Pells's career.

Jonathan became a drunk that year and lost everything. But then he met Muriel Lake and married her. Alice remembered it well. Both Pells and Lake had been her authors; Jonathan was big, Muriel had been small fry. But something in little Muriel had appealed to wounded Jonathan, when nothing or nobody else did.

Alice remembered how she'd learned about the romance. She'd invited him to a book party, and Jonathan and Muriel had shown up as a couple. Muriel hadn't been invited, Jonathan had taken her as his date, and she'd been dressed all wrong. Alice closed her eyes and relived the scene: that form-fitting, imitation-silk suit, whorehouse red. God, how Muriel's buttocks had bounced in it.

Alice had pulled Jonathan off into a corner and asked, straight-faced, "Jonny, are you tutoring now?" But Jonathan hadn't gotten the insult.

"Al, she's going to be great," he'd said. "Her next book, *The Blonde Was All in Red*, it's going to be a wow."

He was already in love with Muriel and he couldn't have known her more than two weeks. Both were writers without a cent to their names or any realistic hope of a future—they had had a blazing hot affair. Oh, how I envied it, Alice thought behind lidded eyes. Both broke, they had danced in the face of misfortune, married on nothing, threw their last thousand dollars into a party and then gotten on with their lives.

For one of them, for Jonathan, the hole had only deepened. He'd had to sign away every penny he'd ever make on *Emily* to the town he'd slandered, and after the court pronounced the whole book a fabrication, there hadn't been any money to speak of. And then no reputable publishing house would have anything to do with him. Jonathan went into the dumper, straight down the neck of a brandy bottle.

Muriel's life took a different turn. Her dinky little novel, *In Dire Extremis*, went to the movies, starring Roland Boland. He won an Oscar and Muriel had her first million after taxes.

The *Emily* case had taken two and a half years before it was finally decided, and for the past three years Gordon had been struggling to make up what had been lost. And if Alice didn't find the manuscript of *Unforgivable Sin*, Haunting House might still go under. Tout Livres wanted Haunting House now, and a Herr Riddleshall of Munich was coming over to tender an offer next week. Alice shuddered. Tout Livres was an international conglomerate. It was very rich and very successful with mass-market magazines, but it had a terrible literary reputation. Now they were making movies, and they wanted their own script factory. That was what they meant to do to Haunting House. If Herr Riddleshall took over, there would be no place for Alice. But Tout Livres hadn't won yet.

Muriel always submitted her manuscripts in blue boxes; Alice opened the walk-in closet door. Ten different padded hangers of clothes, all Muriel's were lined up, shrouded in plastic see-through bags. Pinned to the bags were the day and time when each particular dress or suit was to be worn. Above them on the shelf were shoes on top of shoe boxes, and in the shoe boxes were the accessories Muriel had planned to wear with each outfit, down to hosiery and a decoration for her hair. Alice pushed back the hanger to see what Muriel would have worn today. A soft yellow coat-dress with amber buttons. Lovely. Far beyond Alice's budget. Yes, little Muriel had learned. From too-tight markdowns to beautifully coordinated ensembles, the little girl from Canton, Ohio, had learned how it was done.

On the other side of the closet were two hangers, obviously delegated to Jonathan. One held his dinner jacket and trousers; the other held the corduroy suit and shirt he'd worn yesterday. Whatever he was wearing today summed up his total wardrobe for the five-day convention.

There were no blue boxes in the closet.

Alice turned her attention to the dressers and pulled open the drawers, starting from the bottom. She left them open as she went, not caring that her prying would be obvious. But no blue box, no manuscript.

She opened the suitcases under the bed and looked in every nook and cranny of the sitting room. No five-hundred-page manuscript.

The maid was finally finished in the bathroom. She was a handsome mulatto woman with gold beads in an intricate hairdo. "All set, honey," she said. "I've left you some extra mints, too, on the bed table."

"Thanks," Alice responded and, on impulse, handed the woman a five-dollar bill.

"Oh, no, honey, that's too much. You tip at the end of your stay, and you leave it in your own room. That's how we expect it."

Alice shook her head. "This is just because I feel lucky today. I want you to be lucky, too."

"I thank you for it then." The bill disappeared into the maid's pocket. "I may get lucky," she said as she entered the hall. "There's a new boy workin' here I got to keep my eye on."

"Oh, I hope you get him," Alice said.

"Get 'im?" The maid laughed, placing the cleansers and dirty towels into her cart. "It's gettin' away from him's the problem. It ain't my love he's after, honey. It's information. Murder information." And then she laughed grandly and rolled her cart away, the beads in her hair tinkling.

Amazing, Alice thought. She knew all the time that I didn't belong to this room. She glanced down at her wristwatch. The seminar in which she was to participate started in ten minutes. She hastened into the bathroom and opened all the cabinet doors but found nothing. Well, there was nothing for it. She'd have to ask Jonathan. She had hoped to avoid asking Jonny anything about Muriel's writing, ever.

And then as she stood, undecided, chewing her lip, Jonathan was there in the open bathroom doorway. "Why, hello," he said. "Fancy our meeting again like this."

He looked tired, worn out, but sober. And still younger than his years in his open-throated shirt over a dark green sweater. There was the faintest of gleams in his eye, reminiscent of the way he had looked at her before Muriel had stolen him away. Alice stared, wanting him to make the first move, wanting to loosen the cool china buttons on her ivory blouse. She lifted her hand to the top one under the rolled silk collar.

"You're supposed to be downstairs," he said, his eyes on her upraised hand. "I looked for you. When you didn't show..." He shrugged and took a step into the little room. It smelled of disinfectant and castile soap.

Yes, I hated Muriel, Alice thought. Yes, I'm glad she's gone. "I know you loved her terribly," she said. "I'm so sorry."

"Did I?" he took another step toward her. Barely four feet separated them. Either could close it.

"I loved her, too," Alice lied.

"I wrote *Desperate*," Jonathan said, as softly as though he were making love. "We put her name on it because she was hot and I couldn't have gotten a contract if I'd written the Bible. Then I wrote *Unforgiv-*

able Sin. And Mu said that had to have her name on it, too, to be a hit. I wanted dual authorship, but she nixed it. Said Gordon wouldn't take her if I was part of the package. Put my name back on it for me, Al. It belongs there. And I've a new one, half written, the best yet." He closed the distance between them and put his hand over Alice's uplifted hand, which quivered around her top button.

Her mind whirled. She should get downstairs. Start talking about buying mysteries to eager authors. She should have *Unforgivable Sin* in her hands. She should ask Jonathan where the manuscript was. She should rip open her blouse. She should let him carry her to his newly made bad. There was no trace of Muriel on those fresh, sweet sheets. . . .

"I'll help you, Jonny," she said. His mouth just touched her mouth. She kept talking, speaking the words from her mouth into his. "We'll make it up to Haunting House for *Emily*. You'll come back bigger and better than you ever were."

"I should have married you," he said, "shouldn't I have?"

Her fingers moved then, freeing the button from its silken noose. He pulled at the second one and she slipped the third.

At last, she thought. At last. Whatever I've done, whatever I'm going to do, he's worth it. . . .

She let him ease her down to the tiles of the bathroom floor.

EIGHT

"NOW REMEMBER, Kevin, I want to take notes, so don't talk to me during this seminar, please," Cecilia Burnett whispered. "Not a word."

"Right," Kevin said. "I want to hear, too. But can't we talk before it starts? Alice Ludlow isn't even here yet."

Gordon Gates was in his place in the first chair of five before the unlit fireplace in Ballroom A, which all of the WOM members now referred to as "the scene of the crime." To Gates's right was the notorious bookcase, already photographed by a tabloid newspaper photographer and a national magazine man. At four o'clock, seven television networks were coming and various writers would be spontaneously interviewed on camera. Everyone hoped to be selected by at least one interviewer to give an interpretation of their colleague's untimely death.

Previously that hour had been scheduled as a "tea time cozy," which meant free time for the writers who didn't choose to go on a tour of Manhattan's prison on Rikers Island. But there would be no coziness at today's tea, with the television cameras whirring. And, of course, everyone who had signed up for Rikers had withdrawn. Herman Patrick was supposed to re-schedule the prison jaunt, but he had announced that he wasn't going to do so. He wanted to enjoy the convention as much as the next man, he said; as executive secretary he would waste the remainder of the day negotiating with bureaucrats to reschedule the tour. But he had no intention of missing the action at the hotel, and therefore he canceled the outing.

To Gordon's left, Stanislas Yarrow, the thriller writer, sat with a leg crossed comfortably upon a knee, irritating the already-harassed publisher by jiggling the free foot and coming constantly, perilously, close to cuffing Gates's suit pants. On Stash Yarrow's other side sat Deirdre Day Tully, regal in black. She spoke directly into the ear of Stash Yarrow, who, bent toward her, seemed to be enjoying what he was hearing, for he nodded whenever she paused for breath and didn't interrupt.

The fourth chair was meant for Alice Ludlow and was empty. The fifth held the commanding presence of Augustus Graves, formidable head of Tombstone Books and the man considered the most audacious mind in mystery publishing. Augustus Graves had the ability of being able to make whatever happened in the world suit his current booklist. It was said that he could take any item of fact, however insignificant, and turn it into a newshook for any book he cared to promote. And he cared to promote almost all of his books. He also had the reputation of dropping authors if their books didn't immediately find an audience.

So while Cecilia Burnett, sitting midroom on a settee with Kevin, wanted very much to introduce herself to her publisher, she wasn't brave enough. She told herself it would not be appropriate at this time under the melancholy circumstances.

Augustus Graves, easily into his sixties, had a head of flowing white hair, which he combed straight back and let fly. And while he wasn't handsome, he was tall and broad of girth and shoulder. Cecilia thought his rugged face seemed wise, with strength of character. And it was not only Cecilia who he intimidated. No one from the audience was speaking to him, nor did anyone at the panel attempt to make conversation. He was on the far end of the speaker's line with an empty chair between him and DDT, sitting in splendid isolation, reading galleys of an author's work.

Muriel Lake had been posted as seminar leader, but as that was now impossible, Herman Patrick's plump friend had been given the stand-in honor. Cecilia had forgotten his name, but she watched him as he stood before the window beside the fatal bookcase. He waited impatiently for a signal from Herman to begin.

Cecilia didn't respond to Kevin's plea for conversation. She shifted her gaze to observe the other writers' reactions to the news of Muriel Lake's death. She recorded her observations in her notebook as fast as she could write.

"Most odd," she wrote. "No one is sad. Everyone is stunned, yes, but excited and exhilarated. Gordon Gates seems angry. Or maybe *peeved* is the better word. Well, he has lost a wonderful writer. But even my two new friends, JoAnn Morris and Gilda Shapiro, aka JoAnn M. S. Gold, are chattering away as if nothing has happened. And DDT, at breakfast, actually table-hopped to tell as many of us as she could that she had to hand it to Lady Lake. Muriel sure knew how to throw a party, after all. Incredibly bad taste, but no one rebuked her, certainly not I. Everyone, of course, is saying it's murder and that her husband did it. Stash Yarrow admitted to Detective Scott and the magazine reporter that he had once had an affair with Muriel. DDT overheard and told us. Then DDT said the only reason Stash had kissed and told was to get his name in the news—"

"My God!" Kevin interrupted. "They're starting and Alice Ludlow's not here. Maybe she's been murdered, too!"

Cecilia looked up from her notebook. The moderator was introducing the panelists, and Alice Ludlow's chair was still empty. Cecilia looked at her new friend. Kevin shrugged and took her hand. It was her writing hand, and so she pulled it back and placed his firmly on his own knee.

The room settled down to listen to the advice they had gathered to hear. But Cecilia, try as she might, couldn't concentrate on the words. Her eyes were riveted on the deadly bookcase as she tried to see how it could have happened. Accidentally happened. But she saw that if the heavy piece began to tip, a step toward the window easily put one out of danger. Even if one were climbing on it, there would be time. The case would sway and right itself; it was heavier at the back than at its front. And then, twisting to take in more of the room, Cecilia saw the tall clock and remembered the mysterious tolling last night and the crash. That was it! she thought. I heard it as it was happening, right below me. If I'd gone down, I might have saved her. She wanted to tell someone, tell everyone. But Stanislas Yarrow was speaking.

"Find your worst nightmare," he was saying. "It takes finding. It isn't easy. But when you've got it, then expand it to terrorize the world. That's how you write an international thriller. You take the worst scenario and follow it to its terrible conclusion...."

Murder, thought Cecilia Burnett. It's true, what the others are saying. Muriel Lake was murdered. Frantic, she looked around at the assembled. Both Alice Ludlow and Jonathan Pells were missing. Cecilia stood up and pushed past the chairs toward the doors. She wasn't going to have a second murder on her conscience. She was going to find Alice before it was too late....

But Detective Scott barred her way. "No one leaves this room until I've made my announcement," he said.

"Miss Ludlow," Cecilia said softly, trying to explain without disrupting the discussion up front.

Detective Scott took her arm and sat her down in the chair by the door. "Stay," he commanded her.

Cecilia stayed, but she didn't hear a word of Gordon Gates's or Augustus Graves's advice. She became aware that Deirdre Day Tully laughed appreciatively at her own wit, that Stanislas Yarrow enjoyed the sound of his own voice, that Gordon Gates didn't like Augustus Graves and that Augustus Graves, alone of the panelists, was in shock at Muriel's death. And there must have been a draft where the double doors met because she felt, throughout the discussion, ghostly fingers tingling the back of her neck as though trying to tell her something.

Detective Scott made his announcement when the last question, a query on how an author could help himself gain reader recognition, was answered by DDT's callous "Get yourself killed!"

"I must officially inform you all," he said, "that until you hear differently, none of you is to leave this hotel on any pretext, under any circumstances. You're all, collectively, under suspicion in the death of Muriel Lake at least until the medical examiner releases the cause of death. You're free to call your relatives or attorneys, if you wish, but please keep your comments to the press to a minimum. Dr. Song will address you at dinner with as full a report as he'll be able to present. Are there any questions?"

A hand was raised, and Gilda Shapiro stood up. "Where's Jonathan Pells?" she asked.

"And where's Alice Ludlow?" Cecilia shouted, and felt, distinctly, the ghostly hands fall away.

And then, as if on cue, the ballroom's double doors opened and Jonathan Pells and Alice Ludlow appeared, his hand on her shoulder.

The room erupted in pandemonium. The word *murderer* slithered through the room. And then the second accusation whipped behind it: *mistress*.

"This is just *too* much!" Deirdre Day Tully brayed.

NINE

GORDON GATES SAT despondently in the Franklin Delano Roosevelt Suite with Alice Ludlow and Jonathan Pells. All of Muriel's suitcases, and Jonathan's single one, had been gone through. Her Mercedes in the hotel garage had been checked; the trunk, under the seats, even the glove compartment. *Unforgivable Sin* couldn't be found. Detective Scott had dispatched a man, by telephone, to the Lake estate in Riverdale to search the house, but the officer hadn't, as yet, called in.

"All right, where is it, Pells?" Gordon sighed. "I'll give you whatever you want. An introduction to it, how's that? And your name on the cover under hers."

"Muriel handled everything," Jonathan said. He very much wanted a drink. "It was her contract. She was the boss. I wrote my draft, passed it over to her, she rewrote to suit herself, and it went out of my mind. I passed her my copy and diskette eight months ago. I don't even remember what the damn thing was about. Murder of a child, I think. A woman suspected of killing her baby. Only she didn't do it. The kid's little sister did. Listen, Gor, that book was okay, but I've got another one half written that's better. It's about a young German seamstress during World War II. She makes pillowcases for Hitler—he wants a new one every night. She eventually realizes he uses her pillow patterns to decide his battle strategies. She hates Hitler, but the man she loves is a Nazi and she's stuck in Hitler's entourage. Her lover is the one who tells her that when she uses blue thread, German troops attack from the left, when she uses red, they go right. That sort of thing. He begins telling her what colors to use in her pillowcases. The lover begins plotting the war. And she has to make a pillowcase each night. One day she escapes, gets to an American general—I've made it Eisenhower—tells him the next day's battle plan, which will mean the death of her lover. But she can't bear her betrayal, so she goes back to Hitler's bunker and tells her lover what she's done. He shoots her, she dies in her lover's arms, and they're all destroyed.''

"It sounds magnificent," Alice breathed. "What's it called?"

"*The Himalayan Pattern*," Jonathan answered. "And Muriel's never seen it. She doesn't know it exists. It's all mine."

No one corrected his use of the present tense.

"I don't want *The Himalayan Pattern* or any other work by you, Pells," Gordon said. "I want your late wife's *Unforgivable Sin*. Turn it over or I'll sue the socks off—"

"You forget," Jonathan interrupted. "Socks are about all I have."

"Not now," Alice said, and both men looked at her. "Well, don't you inherit?"

Jonathan shrugged. "I don't know and I don't care."

"Of course you know, you lummox," Gordon stormed. "Are you such an incompetent you don't even know if your wife had a will?"

Jonathan shook his head. "If she did, I never saw it. Anyway, I don't intend to live off Muriel's—"

"Get me that manuscript. That's all I have to say to you. Alice, we're getting out of here. We're going back to the office."

"We can't, Gordon," Alice said in her gentlest voice. "Don't you remember? We're confined to the hotel until Detective Scott says we can go."

"All right, let's just go. I can't stand 'little' novelists. Never could, never will."

"Jonathan's not a little novelist, Gordon." Alice stood to leave and looked at Pells with winsome eyes. "I'll work with you on *The Himalayan Pattern*," she said. "And Gordon will publish it with fanfare. Or I'll leave him. That's a promise."

"Like hell's going to freeze over anytime soon," Gordon said, already at the door.

"If you'd rather, Jonathan and I will go to Tombstone," Alice threatened. "In fact, I think we ought to. We'll be treated better."

Gordon looked at Jonathan, slumped on the side of the bed. "If only it'd been you," he said. "You the world could live without."

Jonathan nodded and reached in his bed table drawer for his brandy flask. "It's just hitting home," he said. "She's really dead, isn't she?" And then he began to cry.

"Oh, spare me," Gordon snarled, and slammed the door on the two of them.

TEN

12:30-1:30 p.m., Wednesday

DETECTIVE SCOTT TOOK the call in his hotel room. "It's not a job I relish," he said, and then, "I'll start right now." He disconnected and called Herman Patrick's room. "Come to my room immediately," he said, "room 413. Bring me the list of attendees and don't tell your friends where you're going."

Herman Patrick was there in three minutes, a typed list in his hand and a portable recording device.

"Sit down," Scotty said, "and tell me what you did last night after dinner." He took the list out of Herman's hand and set it aside.

"Glad to," Herman said, flashing slightly yellow teeth. "I'm going to tape this if you don't mind." Not waiting for an answer, he bent over the controls and pushed a button. A red light appeared and Herman pointed the machine at himself. "I went to the Gardenia Room with just about everybody else. Sat with a group of other writers and talked shop. Went to bed about one. I didn't see Muriel or Jonathan, but then I didn't expect to. Muriel doesn't drink—excuse me, didn't drink—and didn't much socialize after hours, at least not in groups. They say she was better one-on-one. And Jonathan avoids barrooms on occasions like this when he's on the wagon. If he's off, as he apparently is this week, he drinks in his room. Brings his own bottles in. It's cheaper, and what people don't know they don't gossip about. No, I didn't hear anything and I didn't think anything. We're all adults here. This isn't the Girl Scouts. Next question."

"Did you like her?" Scotty watched the stout man's face, the mild blue eyes, the bushy red beard fluffed around a strong jawline, the high forehead.

Herman answered into the grid of his machine. "Muriel was a star in our organization. I couldn't afford not to like her."

"And if you could have?"

Herman dropped his eyes and scratched his beard. "Oh, I don't know. Can this be off the record?" He shut off his own machine and said confidingly, "I didn't really know her personally. Didn't want to. A woman like that is dangerous. I wanted to stay on her good side and stay out of her hair and that's what I did. That's as far as I thought about it."

"What do you mean, 'a woman like that'?"

Herman looked the detective in the eye and snapped on his recorder. "She had hot pants," he said right into it.

"You know that for a fact?"

Herman shrugged. "It was her reputation. I never went to bed with her, if that's what you mean. Muriel didn't go for guys like me."

"What kind of guy is that?"

Herman snapped off the machine. "Look at me," he said. "I'm ordinary, dull, only modestly successful. An overweight drudge who doesn't dress well. I don't do trendy things like the rhumba or travel, and I spend my nights in my hole, writing. I scratch when I itch, eat spaghetti out of cans and drink beer before I go to bed. I'm not the kind of man Muriel invited to come up and see her sometime."

"Okay," Scotty said. "What kind of guy did Miss Lake go for?"

Herman thumbed the recorder on, repeated the detective's question into it and replied for posterity. "Lookers. Big shots. Stash Yarrow, they say. Anybody who could help her get ahead. Or a handsome waiter for a one-night stand. I guess Jonathan just didn't satisfy." He chuckled meanly and then said, "Oops. Shouldn't have recorded that snicker."

"You're smarter than you look, Patrick," Scotty said, moving around his room, touching a room service card, then an advertisement for rental cars.

"Always have been," Herman agreed. The tape purred on.

"Confidentially—" Scotty parked himself against the desk "—what did the other writers think of Muriel, not as a writer, but as a person?"

"You mean did anybody hate her enough to kill her?"

"Exactly."

"Nah," Herman said. "What's to hate? Some of us might have liked to be as successful as she was, but we all want to crack our own safe, know what I mean? Sure, Muriel was cooking, but we all think we'll be the next big log in the fireplace. That's the way writers are—pretty full of themselves, bless our hearts.''

"This is confidential,'' Scotty said. Herman popped the machine and waited expectantly. "Everybody will know it by tonight, but you're knowing it first.''

Herman Patrick smiled.

"It wasn't an accident. I just got the word from the doctor.''

Herman nodded. "Of course not,'' he said. The tape was on again. "It had to be murder.''

"If you know so much, then who did it?'' Scotty asked, suddenly irritated and wondering why.

"That's another easy one,'' Herman said. "Jonathan did it, foolish boy. He found out he was losing his meal ticket. After all, she announced the divorce in front of everybody. He'd been drinking since check-in and maybe before that. I wouldn't be surprised if he clobbered her with that gavel I left in their suite. Do you know about that? It was pretty heavy and had silver facing on squared-off butt ends. A handy little mallet. They fought at dinner, ruined your speech, carried it on in their rooms, then went down to the library to settle it, someplace where they wouldn't be disturbed, where she could lock them in—she had a key remember—and have it out. He lost his temper— Jonathan's good at that—started swinging away, probably connected harder than he meant to, realized he'd killed her and turned over the bookcase to fake an accident. Child's play figuring that one out, Detective Scott. Ask me something hard."

"Okay," Scotty said, half amused, half disgusted. "Who was Muriel leaving him for?"

Herman Patrick combed his beard with his free hand. "Damned if I know," he said after a pause. "But you're right. Muriel wouldn't have left one man until she had another hooked and netted." He stroked his beard faster. "Let's try this one on, shall we, just for fun. How about you?"

"No," Scotty said. Too quick, he thought. I should have relaxed first, stayed with the joke....

"Ah. While the detective checks out everyone's alibi, who checks his?" Herman's hand fell away from his beard, stroking the strap of his little machine.

"Okay, you're excused, Mr. Patrick."

"I bet I am," Herman said. He shut off the recorder, looped it over his pudgy wrist and lifted himself out of the chair. Then he shook his legs to get the wrinkles out of his trousers and straightened his tie in the vestibule mirror. "Just in time for lunch, too. Lucky me."

"Will you send Stanislas Yarrow in, if you can find him?"

"Delighted," Herman answered. "But before I go I have a question of my own."

"Shoot."

"All of us are dying to know. Will the murderer strike again?"

Scotty didn't answer. By the time he had thought of a reply, Herman Patrick was gone.

ELEVEN

DETECTIVE SCOTT OPENED his door to the solid knock, but it wasn't Stanislas Yarrow who stood in the doorway. He looked into the eyes of a thin young woman of pale complexion and wavy auburn hair. She was drably dressed in a long skirt with schoolgirl pleats and a green sweater—that was too large for her—over a round-collared white blouse. She wore low-heeled shoes and dark socks, and except for a wristwatch, no jewelry of any kind. She might have been beautiful. There was symmetry in her features, her eyes were greener than her sweater and her lips were plump and pouty. But she wore no makeup to bring her allure to life, and so presented a rather plain appearance.

"I'm Cecilia Burnett," she said, extending a long-fingered hand. "And I heard the accident happen last night. My room is 444, directly above the ballroom—"

"Come in," he said, releasing her hand and gesturing inside.

"Yes, all right." She had a notebook clutched to her breast, reminding him again of a schoolgirl. She pirouetted once inside, taking in the room, and then stood before him, waiting for permission to sit.

"I'm expecting a visitor," he said, "so I can't give you much time."

"Oh, I've nothing much to say," she said. "I just heard the clock strike and then the crash. Nothing else. But I thought you ought to know."

"Sit," he said. "You mean you can pinpoint the exact time the bookcase fell?"

"I think so." She sat, smoothing her skirt under her, feet close together, and opened her notebook. "I'm the new volunteer recording secretary of WOM. My first book came out last August, so I've just joined."

"Congratulations," he said, and wondered how old she was. Older than she looked probably.

"Thank you," she said. "It didn't set the world on fire."

Yes, he thought, held by her face. With a little sophistication she would be gorgeous.

"I'm a compulsive diarist and note-taker," she said. "That's how I can be so sure."

He looked away from her. "What is it you heard?"

"At midnight, just as I was going to bed, a clock struck from somewhere twelve times. I counted. I completely forgot about the grandfather clock in the library downstairs, so, you see, I don't catch everything. I was more interested in the people last night, I guess—the other writers. So I was bewildered when it tolled and wondered where it came from. It was spooky, although I admit I've got an overvivid imagination. Well, novelists do. We have to." She faltered and looked at him appealingly.

"You heard the clock strike and then the bookcase fall," he prompted.

"Yes," she said solemnly, and rushed on. "But I didn't investigate. That's the awful thing. I was tired and undressed, ready for bed, but I might have saved Miss Lake if I'd gone down to the library. Remember what you said last night in your talk about the things that happen before a crime being telltale, being more important than what happens after?"

"Yes," he said, not remembering. The speech had been a disaster. Even he hadn't listened to what he'd said with Muriel and Jonathan spitting at each other. And he'd forgotten his order and left out half.

"Well," she said. "I met Miss Lake for the first time yesterday morning. I was too early for check-in and met her in the coffee shop, the—" she checked her notebook "—Day Lily, it's called."

"And?"

"And the significant thing that happened then, I think, was that Miss Lake was surprised to see her publisher and editor come in. No, more than surprised. She was disturbed and unhappy."

Scotty sat on the bed, the only other place. "How do you know that?" He wondered if this pretty woman who insisted on being plain was a habitual liar or someone who manufactured facts to suit her purpose or, that rarity, an accurate witness of everyday events. It came to him in immediate insight: he didn't trust women.

Cecilia turned back several pages of her notebook, found the place she wanted and said, "I won't read it out. I'll just paraphrase. When Gordon Gates and Alice Ludlow appeared, Muriel groaned 'Oh, no' and went white. They came over. I excused myself, so I don't know what happened after and didn't see her again until she made that embarrassing announcement about divorcing Mr. Pells." Cecilia looked solemn. "And that announcement was very strange, too, I think, don't you? Not the way it's usually done."

He shrugged. "Muriel liked the limelight. It didn't seem strange to me that she would find a newsworthy way to let the world know what she was up to. She was good at that, getting attention. She did it a lot."

"Oh, well, then." Cecilia stood up. "That's really all I can tell you. I hope it helps. Oh, and maybe one other thing. Miss Lake's death was no accident. It was either murder or suicide. I'm sure of that."

"Are you now?"

"Yes." She was heading for the door. "After everyone left the library this morning, I tried it, and it can't be done. Not with my weight and I'm heavier than Miss Lake. I'm taller, which spreads the weight some, I grant you, but Kevin and I both tried, and we agreed."

Scotty followed her to the door. "What did you try?"

"Why, overturning the bookcase. I climbed it the way the story's being told she did, and it didn't budge. Then Kevin stood on the second shelf, and he weighs one-sixty. With me on it, it didn't even tremble. With Kevin the shelf almost broke. So it's not possible, is it?''

"Maybe not," Scotty said, and reached in front of her to open the door. "Maybe you're right there, miss."

"Well. Goodbye."

Stanislas Yarrow was coming out of the elevator. He saw Cecilia Burnett and waited, holding the elevator door open for her. She stepped in and faced front. She was smiling at the thriller writer as though he made her heart beat quicker.

TWELVE

SCOTTY WAITED until Stash Yarrow had closed the door, then said, "I'm going to miss my lunch if I don't get down there. Had yours?"

"Just finished," Yarrow confirmed. "But I'll go with you if you'd like. Have another coffee and explain myself. I assume that's what you want of me."

"Let's go." Scotty closed his door and headed for the exit stairs.

Almost all of the WOM participants were sitting at the tables in Ballroom B. They were talking intensely together, chattering, laughing. A few were smoking. Some already had drinks; others lingered over dessert and coffee. For a moment Scotty envied them. They could afford to entertain themselves at Muriel's expense. He couldn't.

He found a vacant table. "I'll be right back as soon as I fill my plate," he said to Yarrow. "Will you chase away anybody who tries to sit with us?"

"Sure." The thriller writer sat and stretched out his legs. "I had the turkey tetrazzini. Wasn't bad."

Scotty headed for the buffet table determined to eat anything except the turkey tetrazzini. He chose macaroni and cheese, which he hadn't had in years. He found some bread and a diet cola and headed back to the table, hating Stash Yarrow, hating himself. Jonathan was sitting there, opposite Yarrow. Jonathan's plate was full of turkey tetrazzini.

"Hope you don't mind," Jonathan said. Yarrow shrugged helplessly. "Old friends and all that. We who spent a night with Muriel and survived to tell about it. We must start a made-for-profit organization."

"I'll just get myself a cup of coffee," Yarrow said, and eased himself away.

"I think of poor Muriel in bed with that cardboard ninny and I just feel sorry for her," Jonathan said. "What some women will do in the name of liberty."

"I got the call from the medical examiner," Scotty said, sitting down. "It wasn't an accident. She was hit twice by the same instrument. The bookcase couldn't have killed her, because any one corner couldn't have been in two different places at the same time. Unless some gorilla dropped it on her once, lifted it while she tried to crawl away and dropped it down again. She was hit with something blunt-edged and very heavy. When I suggested a gavel, Dr. Song said no, unless the gavel had knobs on it at least four inches thick and maybe fifty pounds.... Did it?"

Jonathan said nothing. Probably had a fifth of brandy by now, Scotty thought and sighed. "I've been assigned the case," he said. "I'm questioning Mu's friends—"

"Muriel had no friends," Jonathan interrupted. "Just people she could use. Some of us are like that."

"I was Muriel's friend," Scotty replied.

"Mu laughed at you behind your back. Whatever she wanted to know, you told her for free. You were a chump. You could have gotten money."

Scotty watched the cheese cool and stiffen on his plate. "I would have told you, too, if you asked."

"Yeah, maybe. If I'd held your dick the way she did."

"You make it hard to be nice." The macaroni and cheese was good.

"You know, it's funny," Jonathan said. "I'm glad she's gone. Terrible thing to admit, but it's true. I loved her for a while, sure, but I never really liked her."

"Hell," Scotty said, embarrassed. He wanted to say, "Anything you say can and will be used against you in a court of law," but he didn't. Instead he said, "You were nuts about her. I remember—"

Jonathan's cheeks were full again. He raised a finger, wagged it and said before he swallowed, "That was at the beginning, chum. Before I knew better."

Yarrow had returned, but Scotty couldn't help himself. He said to Pells in a quiet rage, "What in God's holy name did Mu ever do to you? She supported you. She kept your dirty secrets—"

"She stole my work. That's what she did. She took my publisher, used my talent and bad luck to help herself and then she stole my work."

"Justifiable homicide, I'd say," Stash Yarrow announced, steam from the coffee cup he was holding giving his face a shine. "But I think I'll leave you now. You two obviously want to be alone."

Neither man paid him any attention. They leaned across the table toward each other, and Scotty said, "Now we're getting down to it, you slimy bastard. *Evil in Emily*. That was Mu's fault, right? All those lies you wrote. That was all Mu's doing, none of yours."

Jonathan laughed in Scotty's face. "No, you jerk. *Evil in Emily* was all mine before I knew Muriel Lake existed. I wrote it as a piece of fiction and then got the idea to make it a real town, make it a supposed exposé. Towns don't sue, I thought. They just ban you and get you lots of publicity. Okay, I was wrong. But I paid for that, pal, in spades. *Emily*'s gone and forgotten. Now I'm on a comeback, and Mu's dying isn't going to stop me. And you're not going to stop me. Because I had nothing to do with Mu's death. Absolutely nothing."

Scotty couldn't understand his anger, but it was controlling him, driving him. "You fought with her last night," he said, managing to keep his voice down. "It was probably because of you that she went down to that room to get some peace. You were drunk. You could have followed her down, knocked her out and pulled over the bookcase." The macaroni was cold now, and he wanted to eat. And he wanted to scream and hit and hit.

"I could have, Scotty, but I didn't, and you know I didn't," Jonathan answered calmly. "I told you. I went to bed. I acted up because she cut my balls off in front of everybody, announcing a divorce like that. Shit! I knew she wanted out, but I never expected it to come that way. I knew she was planning something, though. I could always tell when Mu was cooking up some scheme she didn't want me to know about. And she was seeing somebody. I know that, too. There's been somebody steady for the past six months, somebody who mattered. I thought it might be you. Maybe it was you.''

Scotty sneered into his macaroni.

Jonathan continued. ''Mu was acting out a script she'd written in her head. She wanted me to fight with her. It fitted into her plan. And like a dummy I fell into the trap again. The whole thing started Monday, really. Monday night she packed and left the house. Told me she couldn't take me anymore, that I was a has-been and she was going all the way to the top— alone. I was an impediment. She didn't love me anymore. I should realize that and do the right thing, not fuss, not stand in her way. Then she left. I never laid a hand on her. I poured myself a drink. Seven months sober and I fell off the wagon. Okay, and here's why— I realized Mu was right. It would be better if we ended it. We'd used each other up. I'd have to walk away from all the comfort I'd gotten used to, but I could do that. Comfort's a woman's game, anyway. It shook me, scared me. I was going to have to start over one more time at the grand old age of fifty-five, with nothing to show for my life except a paid-for computer, a roll of printout paper and a drinking problem. So I had another drink to help me face the demons. I didn't act like a gentleman yesterday. I was stupid and ill-bred and ill-mannered and all those things I really am. But I didn't kill Mu. I swear, Scotty, I never laid a hand on her in anger. Ever.''

"Somebody did," Scotty said. The rage was gone from him now. Now what he felt was shame. He pushed away from the table and left the friend he didn't know anymore.

Stanislas Yarrow was at a large table surrounded by admirers. Scotty signaled to him. With a remark Scotty couldn't hear, he excused himself and came smiling, as though bestowing a blessing on Scotty by his attention. The detective took the author's elbow and guided him to the elevator. Yarrow obviously didn't like being handled, but he didn't protest. He's a smoothie, this one, thought Scotty. Not the kind to risk his neck for a woman. . . .

Back in room 413 Scotty offered Yarrow the chair and said he'd stand. "Just tell me what you know about Muriel Lake, what your relationship was to her, what you think happened. Take your time and try not to leave anything out. That wouldn't be smart."

Yarrow crossed his cream-trousered legs, loosened his brightly patterned silk tie and rested his head against the back of the chair. "Glad to," he began, "and what you must try to understand, Detective Scott, is that writers—creative people—see life differently than normal people do. The average man acts to his own advantage as he sees it, but a novelist purposely doesn't sometimes. We like to create problems just to consider the possibilities. Sometimes we even repeat a particularly juicy conundrum, trying first one script line and then another. Actors do the same thing. They're famous for it. Do you see?''

Scotty, who stood behind the author's back, was looking out the hotel room window. He stared at a cathedral, its fretted spires fired silver at the sun. He saw the Empire State Building, and there were penthouses with overflowing gardens. "How could I?" he said, "I'm not creative."

He was cold in a warm room. He had liked Muriel, admired her, but hadn't loved her. No, he'd never loved her. Then why did he ache so? Where did his sense of shame come from? What did he know that he wasn't telling himself? "Tell me everything," he finally said.

Yarrow sighed. "Bragging in front of an audience comes easily to me. In private it's harder."

Scotty watched a helicopter lumber through the sky.

"Muriel wasn't as successful as I am," Yarrow continued. "That's important to understand. In my world success is the only virtue. Not goodness, not talent, not looks or the clothes you wear, not even the quality of your work. Just success. Any success. But while Muriel wasn't yet my equal, she was making it, she was coming, so she merited attention. The celebrity world is a small one, and an even smaller one in the writing game. In America there's James Michener, Sidney Sheldon, Stephen King, Danielle Steel, me.

A dozen of us, say, give or take one or two at any one time. The kind of success I enjoy comes from a fortress of achievement that's almost fail-proof. Three, four books in a row that went big internationally were made into movies and had paperback sales of over a million. Serious success, commercially speaking. I'm not talking literature. That's a whole other world of little, effete rewards. Literature's not the ball game today. Entertainment is."

"So," Scotty said, still staring at the skyline. *Envy*, he thought. That's what I felt for Muriel. I sensed this specialness he's talking about and I resented it. That's why I wanted to make love to her. It wasn't real desire. I wanted to see her naked, to cut her down to size by laying her, to see her as just another fifty-five-year-old woman. Goddamn me, I was jealous.... "Go on," he told Yarrow. "You interest me."

"Ah, you've seen I'm clever. Good, I'll tell you more. Authors such as myself cause a stir whenever our names are mentioned, whether it's at a garden club or somebody's posh little dinner or within our own circles, for example at this WOM convention. But here's the other side. Our faces aren't widely recognizable. We're not the jet set or the pretty set or corporate tycoons who advertise on television. We're invisible celebs. We need our names pinned on our lapels to attract attention. And like most wishes that the genie grants, author celebrity is a two-edged sword. We like being anonymous when it suits our purpose, but once you've tasted the fruit of the famous-tree, you quickly become addicted. So you seek out others like yourself to play with. And that, not so simply said, is how it was with Muriel Lake and me. She wanted to hobnob one level up. I wanted to fondle no more than one level down. It's safer playing pickup when the other person has something to lose as well as a reputation to protect. And even for a star it's more fun playing house with a name than a nobody, even if her sparkler isn't as bright as yours yet.

"So I saw Muriel on several occasions last year when I was in town. We wined and dined and trysted in various hotel rooms. I liked her—she was a likable woman. When we were done, she went home to her husband with whom she was unhappy but felt a responsibility toward. He had helped her in her career and she was grateful. She wanted to pay him back, wanted to leave him only after he was back on track with a good book. She told me once that she thought Jonathan might have lost the fire in his belly and might be written out. If that was the case, she said, she'd never leave him.

"Bluntly I didn't care what she did or didn't do. She and I were a casual thing. And then I think she fell in love. Because I called her in March when I was in town for some tarty little award or other, and she said she wouldn't come out and cheat anymore, she'd stopped. She said she'd found a way out of her problem. And, no, I didn't ask what problem. I wanted a date not a therapeutic session. She said she'd see me on the talk show circuit. She was putting finishing touches on a new manuscript, and for me to just wait. The prepublication publicity for it would start as soon as she submitted it. That was horsefeathers, I thought at the time. Nothing starts when you turn a manuscript in but rewrites. But Muriel said the advance publicity would start in May at the WOM convention, and it would knock my socks off. Well, I must have spoken my mind on the impossibility of that—you see, I can speak my mind and so often do—and she said, these are almost exactly her words, 'Remember the Agatha Christie brouhaha. You're going to die of jealousy. See you in May. If you miss the fireworks, you'll hate yourself.'"

"What brouhaha?" Scotty had turned away from the window and was now sitting at the desk, staring at the back cover of his autographed copy of *Desperate*. Muriel's face looked up at him from the dust jacket. She was dressed in black against a black background, sitting in an old electric chair. It was a real one pulled out of the penitentiary at Ossining and now in a theatrical company's warehouse. Her golden hair was spread in a spiked halo as though she were being fried, but her face was smiling. The portrait had been airbrushed to remove all facial lines—she was beautiful. The idea for the portrait had been Muriel's. She'd heard about the chair, rented it and went to the warehouse with a photographer and a makeup artist. He and Jonathan had hated the idea, but it had made Muriel's face famous and the photographer had won an award.

Yarrow had been talking again for some time. Scotty hadn't caught any of it. He brought his attention back to what the famous writer was saying.

"It was during the twenties in England when Agatha Christie published her fourth book. She and her husband were at the beginning of the end of their marriage. He'd fallen for his secretary and Agatha was devastated. She ran away from home and was missing for about a week. Her car was found near a lake with the front door open. For a while they thought Archibald had killed her."

"Her husband?" Scotty began breathing faster. He *knew* something, if he could only pull it out of his subconscious.

"Yes, errant Archie. Then Miss Christie was found rather errant herself, dancing the tango at a seaside resort or some such thing. She'd been there a week, registered under her husband's secretary's name and having, apparently, a wonderful time. She said she'd suffered from amnesia and remembered nothing, and she never said anything else about it, at least in public, for the rest of her life. Her disappearance made worldwide news, and her new novel, *The Murder of Roger Ackroyd*, became her first big hit. The publicity did it for her, of course, but the book was very good, very tricky. She chose a good one to launch her career."

"Did you ask Muriel about all that when you saw her yesterday?" Scotty asked.

"No," Yarrow replied. "I'd honestly forgotten about it, since it didn't concern me. But this morning, after I heard the incredible news, I remembered it vividly, and—" he swung his head to see the detective's reaction "—thought I'd be a good citizen and pass along what I could."

"I wonder if it means anything," Scotty muttered. He touched the glossy paper where Muriel's throat disappeared into blackness and tried to see through her eyes. Brown eyes, they had been. Light brown, almost golden.

"Oh, it must," Yarrow shot back.

"Why must it?"

"You haven't been listening, after all, Detective." Yarrow was peevish now. "It must, because of what I've just told you about creative people. Clever people. People who design their futures and act on those designs. People like *Muriel*."

"You mean she planned something and it went wrong?"

"Or it's going marvelously well. Finally it sinks in."

Scotty turned away from Muriel's face and moved around to face Yarrow straight on. "But what? The woman's dead, for God's sake."

"Well, that's your job, isn't it, finding out?" the writer said. "Me, I've got to change for a TV interview downstairs. If you need me, I'll be around. I'm not planning a stunt, at least not this year."

He started to rise, but Scotty pushed him back. "Just one more minute."

Yarrow sank back into the cushions and waited.

"What did you do last night after dinner?"

"I sat in a cocktail room downstairs with Deirdre Day Tully and a would-be writer named Kevin Wilder. I had two campari and sodas. When the company began to bore me, I left. It was about eleven. I took a stroll up the avenue to Central Park, came back and went to bed. I imagine Muriel was getting herself killed while I was out, unfortunately. As far as I know, I saw no one I knew or who knew me on my walk. I didn't see Muriel and heard nothing deadly. Now may I go?"

"They can't find the manuscript," Scotty said. "Muriel's last manuscript is missing."

Yarrow rose. "Of course!" He spread his hands wide as though that explained everything. "That's what we all hear. Well, don't worry, dear dim Detective Scott, they'll find it, one copy or another. There's never only one copy of a manuscript, you see. There'll be one in her safe-deposit box. There'll be one in a closet of her house. It'll be on her computer hard disk or on a copy-protected floppy. The last work of Muriel Lake will surface after a sufficient publicity hunt and be worth its weight in royalty checks. Goodbye for now."

Scotty sat in the chair Yarrow had just vacated. It was warm from the writer's body. He closed his eyes. "Thanks for your help," he said before Yarrow escaped into the hall. "I mean it. You've helped."

"So are we all, all honorable men. Isn't that what Mark Antony said of Caesar's assassins in Shakespeare's play?"

"I don't know," Scotty replied.

"Well, I do."

The writer let himself out.

Publicity stunt, thought Scotty. No, it couldn't be. Muriel is dead. I saw the body, kissed her, for God's sake.

Scotty shuddered. But what if she wasn't?

THIRTEEN

ROMEO POPOI CREPT across the attic of the Hepplewhite where the hotel's upper management were allowed their own rooms. He was finished work for the day and he had the master key, which he hadn't returned to Mr. V. He had learned there was a record room in a far wing of the top floor, a vast loftlike space where all the documents, receipts and records of the Hepplewhite were stored. The head bellman had told him to look for a brown metal door at the top of a flight of stairs. There was no elevator to the record room.

Romeo sought the final flight of stairs, hoping he'd run into no one. If he did, he had his excuse ready. He would say he was looking for the banquet manager in order to return the master key. At lunchtime he'd had a duplicate made, but the Puerto Rican who had cut it had cautioned him that it might not work: "This key an old one, where you get it?"

"My granny's," Romeo had said. "It fits her house."

"My blanks no right, but I try. If key no work, you bring it back, no harm done."

No harm done, thought Romeo, a panic in his belly. No harm done....

He found the flight of stairs behind a rolling screen and climbed them quickly. The floor at the top of the stairs was plain wood and dusty. Down a narrow hall, back along the line of the stairway, he could see a brown metal door. He was in a dormer of the hotel roof. A grime-smeared window looked down upon Fifty-fifth street. Romeo stepped through the dust, leaving tracks.

Eager, he pushed the new key into the keyhole. It went in, wouldn't turn, then wouldn't come out. He cursed and pulled. The key was in and staying in.

He searched his pockets. He had a nail file and a comb, a few coins and the little scrap of paper he had pulled from the notepad in the Franklin Delano Roosevelt Suite. He looked at what it said again: "*Sin* in the library." Then he laughed like the madman he felt himself to be, balled the paper into a knot and tossed it. A good pair of pliers, not junk. That's what he needed now. Pliers, he thought. And butter... He would have to leave the key in and hope that no one came until he returned.

He whirled, decision made, and went quietly back down the stairs and ran along to the elevator. There he hesitated before passing it by. It was safer to take the emergency stairs. In the employees' elevator he'd be trapped. He might be seen leaving it; be remembered. He took the stairs. On the floor below he would take the public elevator. At fifteen he'd have to change elevators down to the main floor. From there he'd use the service stairs to the basement where he was going. Better safe than sorry, he thought. And he could afford the time; he wasn't going anywhere but back up. And if no one discovered the key in the lock, there'd be . . . no harm done.

No harm done.

He ran the stairs to the rhythm of it.

FOURTEEN

EDUARDO VINICI, in his basement office off the kitchen, felt harassed to the breaking point. He had discovered the body of the unfortunate woman, had had to bring in the police, make a statement, worry about getting Ballroom A cleaned up—the police had monopolized it for hours—worry about the damn writers talking to the press and worry about the horde of TV and newspaper people who were descending on the hotel.

And of course at the florists' luncheon, someone who had heard of Muriel Lake's death and had sold an astounding number of funeral bouquets to the WOM writers had then spoken for twenty minutes to the other less enterprising florists on the topic, "Opportunities Are Everywhere." He'd received a standing ovation. So now everyone in the Hepplewhite knew that the death of a famous person had taken place on the premises in mysterious fashion—even the business overnighters and the ladies who lunched. And everyone was calling it murder. Suddenly the not overly famous Muriel Lake had become a major American star, and Mr. V could just see the ghastly headlines: "Horror Hotel."

And then there was Alfredo, the day chef. He was in a royal rage because a truckload of ducks hadn't arrived as promised. The driver had seen two police cars in front of the delivery door, and because the ducks were black market, fresh but not government-inspected, he had turned tail and driven back to Chinatown. And now he refused to return. What was he supposed to serve the mystery writers? Meat loaf? Alfredo had challenged. He'd resign first. So a salad man had been dispatched to Chinatown to pick up the ducks in a Hepplewhite airport van. Mr. V refused to think about what the van would look and smell like after the trip.

His left hand wouldn't stop shaking, and for the first time Mr. Enders, Hepplewhite's general manager, had asked him about it. Mr. Enders was unaware of his banquet manager's black market kickback deal with the Imperial Jade Import-Export Association. If the practice came to light, Mr. V was afraid it would mean prison or at the very least his immediate and permanent retirement.

And now, the last straw, his only spare master key was missing. If he lost control of his master keys, the underlings would steal him blind. They already managed to help themselves when his back was turned.

The new man. Now he remembered. He'd given that skirt-chasing new boy he'd switched out of room service a master key to rouse Muriel Lake's drunken husband from his bed. Willing his hand to stop shaking, Mr. V buzzed the head bellman, Bill Lawrence.

Lawrence, a small man who was getting on in years now, stuck his head through Mr. V's doorless office arch. "Sir?"

Left hand deep in his jacket pocket, Mr. V swung his chair to face the bellman. "This morning I gave my spare master key to your new man...Romeo something. He hasn't returned it and I told him to be sure to. But I've been so busy. I thought he might have left it with you."

"No, and he's gone for the day, Mr. V."

"Are you sure?"

"Well, he signed out at the desk. I could check his punch card if you'd like."

"Please do. If he's gone, don't bother to tell me. Just ask him for it first thing tomorrow. I want it back. But if he's still hanging around somewhere, the workers' cafeteria or employees' lounge, I'd appreciate your sending him in here to me."

"Will do."

"Now that I've got you here, how's he working out?"

The old bellman shook his head. "Don't know yet, Mr. V. Seems okay. Comes when you call. That's about all I noticed in one day. Maybe he likes himself a little too much, pats his hair in front of mirrors, but that's youth, ain't it? Better that way than the other."

"Sorry to bother you with this."

"No trouble."

With a tip of his cap, Bill Lawrence headed back to the main desk, and for an idle moment Eduardo Vinici wished he was more like the bellman. A lifelong bachelor like Mr. V, Lawrence spent all his money on the ponies. He lived without ambition and without laziness. He did his job, enjoyed his leisure, was content. He was sixty-two or sixty-three, two or three years older than Mr. V. He would retire soon, move to Florida, spend his time at the track. He wouldn't be rich, but he'd have enough. He'd have all that he wanted. Not like Mr. V. Mr. V wanted Manhattan after retirement, a social life, fine rooms. Maybe even a pretty divorcée with a summer place in Newport. Why not? Mr. V liked the better things. He had made a career out of his knowledge and appreciation of better things. He fingered the cool petals of the jonquil bud in his lapel: champagne tastes, beer pocketbook. It was a common story....

Out of the corner of his eye he saw the man he'd been looking for. Romeo was slinking out of the kitchen from behind the metal console that held the cold sauces, shrimp, butter and salad greens in ice. Romeo had a paper bag in his hand and was clearly trying not to be seen.

Mr. V got up to chase him. The boy had probably stolen shrimp or some cold ham. Everyone was forbidden to; everyone did a little. It was one of the unresolvable impasses between management, who had the right to eat whatever they wanted, and staff who didn't. The workers felt they, too, should be entitled to eat whatever the kitchen served. After all, so much was simply thrown away. And so the kitchen help and the waiters and any other staff member who had the opportunity, helped themselves to the delicacies. They tried not to get caught and management, within reason, tried not to see.

The boy was taking a service elevator. Mr. V didn't stop him, but he watched the arrow on the indicator as it spun all the way to the top. That elevator didn't go beyond the fifteenth floor. There, another bank of service lifts went all the way to the thirty-third. The penthouse floor was the highest one reserved for guests. The thirty-fourth was for hotel personnel and storage, the thirty-fifth was also storage and the paper attic where the Hepplewhite's records were kept.

Mr. V moved toward another private elevator that was used only by upper management. It serviced the hotel from the thirty-fourth floor to the stockroom basement, and it obeyed only the operator's instructions. While in use it responded to no call from outside or from any floor. And it was the fastest lift; Mr. V kept it greased and running like a Rolls. He would beat the young man to the fifteenth floor, would greet Romeo as he was stepping out, would collect his master key. And then he would face whatever hell was happening between the writers and the press in Ballroom A.

He passed the day chef, sweating before the ovens in his whites. "Even your meat loaf would be better than anything they've had before, maestro," Mr. V said gently as he patted the sensitive man's sleeve.

The chef was much calmer now. "I will carry on, Monsieur V, *merci*. And we will have, after all, our lovely ducks."

Feeling better, Mr. V stepped into his chariot and zoomed the handle for the fifteenth floor.

FIFTEEN

BALLROOM A WAS FILLED with writers, reporters and photographers when JoAnn Morris and Gilda Shapiro, wearing identical leopard-print dresses, made their entrance. They paused for effect in the double doorway after making sure that the book each carried was highly visible. JoAnn carried the first in their Racy Lacy Series, *Ripped!* Gilda cradled their latest, *Hedy Died in Her Teddy*.

The NBC reporter broke off his interview with Herman Patrick in midsentence with "Thanks, buddy, I'll get back to you," and broke for the glamorous pair. He was a handsome Hispanic in tight jeans under a blue suit jacket, white shirt and silk tie. "Raoul, the cleavage!" he shouted to his minicam man, and aimed his microphone at the soft flesh of Gilda's partially exposed chest.

"Gotcha," Raoul crowed, running after the reporter with bent knees to keep the line of vision level.

The woman representing CBS, a cool blonde, ended her conversation with Deirdre Day Tully saying, "Thank you, my dear. I do hope you're wrong." Then she swung in toward the leopard ladies from the other side.

ABC, personified by a sophisticated man with a worldly air about him, moved in on DDT for his turn, but watched his rivals taking the first play away from him again. "Never mind," he said to his camera and audio men. "They get them first, but we get them best." Then be bowed to the shrewd-eyed old woman in black. "I've admired you for years and my wife reads you constantly...."

The bugle beads on Deirdre Day Tully's bodice glimmered, darkened and glimmered. "Muriel Lake got what she deserved," she said.

The NBC man moved closer.

Several other TV networks also worked the room, moving from one writer to another. A national news network had corralled both Gordon Gates and Augustus Graves in front of the infamous bookcase and was happily filming, if not an actual fistfight, then the kind of nasty sound bites that would have to be bleeped when the story was finally aired.

"Your books are the sewage system of the world," Graves was informing Gates. "I offer to buy you out to stop you, not to absorb you."

"You're jealous because I take your writers," Gordon shot back spiritedly, "once they get good." But he was sweating. If Augie Graves mentioned *Evil in Emily*, Gordon swore to himself he'd kick the man into the fireplace.

Herman Patrick, in a high-backed armchair, began his third interview as he had his first. "I write under the nom de plume of Hermione Trick, a woman's name, and I write from a woman's point of view. Muriel admired that. She had trouble with her male characters and she told me what an inspiration I was to her.'' He then reached out and touched the cover of his latest novel, *After a Winter in the Sea*, which stood propped up against the pedestal of the lamp on the table beside him. The camera took the hint and closed in on it. ''We'll all miss her terribly. She was one of our best writers. But, of course, it was an accident, a terrible, terrible accident. Just think of the stories that will never be written now, never be read and enjoyed. I'm making a promise here today—'' the camera dutifully panned back to focus on Herman's solemn face ''—to dedicate my next novel, *Murdered*, to her memory. Somehow I feel she'll be pleased.''

''I think Muriel killed herself,'' the bosomy Gilda was telling both ABC and CBS. ''But she didn't want us to know, didn't want to make us sad. So she gave us a mystery to remember her by, a last chapter you could call it.'' She lifted the book she was carrying so that its cover art couldn't be missed by the camera.

The NBC man asked if she were cold, and Raoul, his cameraman, stood straight and aimed the camera down into her low-cut bodice. ''My books wear jackets. I don't,'' she said, and shifted her weight to make her bosom bounce.

JoAnn Morris, the smaller of the two authors, played straight woman to Gilda's wisecracks. ''I'm still in shock,'' she said. ''I thought Muriel and Jonathan were the book world's happiest couple. To think that he ... well, it's my opinion that Jonathan Pells killed his wife in a rage over her decision to divorce him. I'm sure he's sorry now." Then she turned her book to face the cameras and said, "Muriel told me just yesterday that *Ripped!* was one of her favorite mysteries. It's out in paperback now from Tombstone, and JoAnn M.S. Gold, that's us, will be autographing books at the Creaking Door Bookstore from noon to four tomorrow."

Stanislas Yarrow was talking with a journalist from *Life* magazine, banging his latest book for emphasis on his knee. "Where's her husband? That's what I'm asking myself right now. I'm told he's been allowed to go to their home to look for the missing manuscript. Why haven't you checked him out? If I was writing this as a thriller, Jonathan Pells would long be airborne by this time, the joint bank account would have been cleaned out, and he'd be getting ready to set down in Brazil, where the U.S. hasn't got an extradition treaty. Listen, in my *Peril in Potsdam*, the villain does something much like that. And President Truman's going crazy because the villain has the blueprints to our atomic bomb and is going to deliver them to a representative of Hirohito, who is plotting to blame Roosevelt for Pearl Harbor...."

Cecilia Burnett, unnoticed and unsought, sat on a settee with Kevin Wilder. She was industriously writing down her impressions, Kevin was trying to watch everything at once. "Savages, Ceci, that's what they all are," he said gleefully. "I'm getting a real education."

Cecilia was used to him by now. She wrote on in a swift hand, then paused to say, "Gordon Gates is frantic. He needs a new manuscript immediately, a really good one, to save his company. Unless Muriel's is found, of course. Do you have anything to show him? It could be your chance."

"I have a finished novel, but I'd be afraid to show it to him. Maybe I'm not good enough yet. I'd show it to you, though."

"What if it stinks? What could I say?"

"That it stinks, I suppose. But if it's great, you'd have to say that, too."

"You know, you're not so bad for a nobody, Kevin."

"And I'm handsome, Ceci. Have you noticed that I'm handsome? And I'm as loyal as a dog."

"Let me concentrate on this circus, please. I wish somebody would interview me."

"They won't because you don't make yourself important. You're wearing a boring blouse and skirt and terrible shoes. You look more unpublished than I do. Observe JoAnn M. S. Gold doing their star number and learn, girl. Everyone here but you is polishing his star."

Cecilia thought about it. "I didn't know this was part of writing. Even Herman Patrick's plump friend is getting attention. He's got two reporters all to himself."

"This is what you do," Kevin advised. "Go up to anybody with a microphone and say something sensational. That's what the others are doing."

"Like what? That I know who murdered Muriel Lake?"

"That'd do it."

Cecilia swung her legs and thought about it.

"Okay," Kevin said. "Don't sell any books. I don't care."

"Who would I accuse? Mr. Pells?"

"Honestly, I think Alice Ludlow did it," Kevin said. "She's mad for the new widower. Did you see her this morning, recklessly hand in hand with him? Talk about self-incrimination."

"I think DDT is a possibility." Cecilia put her notebook and pen away in her purse. "I heard at lunch that DDT wrote hate letters to Muriel and even signed her name last year. Muriel sent Herman Patrick copies and asked if he could get her to stop, but he wasn't able to. DDT is like that nine-hundred-pound gorilla who sleeps wherever it wants to—nobody tells her how to behave. She felt snubbed by Muriel and really hated her. She doesn't deny it. And she wouldn't stint at knocking over the furniture."

"I don't think she'd be strong enough," Kevin argued. "Well, maybe if she used a very long broomstick for leverage." A waiter passed near them with hors d'oeuvres on a tray. "Hey, over here," Kevin called, and the CBS reporter, finished with the leopard twins, moved their way. "Oh, my God, here comes

CBS. Say something startling, Ceci. Make some news!''

Cecilia blushed as the microphone leaned toward her chin. ''I'm Starla Meyer, CBS,'' the reporter said. ''Were either of you colleagues of Muriel Lake?''

Kevin shrank back, but Cecilia stood. ''Yes, I am,'' she said. ''Or I was. My book, *Death Wakes Up*, is sold out, so I couldn't find a copy to bring with me today, but I'd like to tell you my theory of what happened to Muriel Lake.''

The reporter waved her cameraman in closer and nodded for Cecilia to continue.

''Muriel Lake was murdered,'' Cecilia said clearly. ''My friend and I tested Detective Scott's hypothesis about her climbing up and pulling the bookcase down on herself, but it won't work that way. Someone purposely hit her and then knocked over the bookcase, but it wasn't her husband. It was the lover she'd gone down at midnight to meet. Her mystery lover.''

Beyond the glowing red eye of the camera, Cecilia saw, bearing down upon her, the publisher of Tombstone Books.

''And who was Muriel Lake's lover?'' the CBS reporter queried. ''Do you have any information on that?''

Cecilia started to say she didn't know. She couldn't concentrate with Augustus Graves coming at her the way he was. Then he stepped into camera range beside her. ''I'll answer for Miss Burnett,'' he said. Then he spoke in a voice loud enough for the whole room to hear: "*I* was Muriel Lake's beloved. I'm the man she had agreed to marry as soon as she was free to do so."

And then he took Cecilia's arm and steered her away. "I've been looking for you all day," he told her, as though he hadn't just silenced the whole room and stolen the show. "I want to tell you how excited I am about your upcoming book."

Cecilia looked up at him, astonished. She had no time to find her voice because they were both immediately surrounded by media representatives barking questions, shoving microphones, aiming their smoldering red-eyed machines at the two of them.

And then someone hollered that Jonathan Pells was in the room and another announced Detective Scott, and Gordon Gates was clawing at the crowd of reporters, trying to get through the circle to Augustus Graves. "The manuscript," Gordon Gates was screaming. "Where's the manuscript?"

Augustus Graves held Cecilia's shoulder with one great, strong hand and raised the other for silence. "All right, you want to know? I'll tell you."

The cameras filmed, the microphones recorded, Gates struggled behind the technicians, who formed a ring to exclude him.

"Earlier this year," Graves said, "I entered into an agreement with Miss Lake to publish her forthcoming novel, *Unforgivable Sin*."

"It's mine," Gates bellowed. "I have that book under contract, you jackal!"

Graves took a deep breath and pressed on. "Miss Lake and I met over the Christmas holidays, renewed our acquaintance—I was her first publisher—and fell deeply in love. We decided upon a course of action, necessarily kept private, and yesterday morning I met Muriel and took possession of the manuscript. Gordon Gates, see your attorney. That's all I have to say at this time."

"Let me at him. I'll kill him. I'll kill him!"

Alice Ludlow sat down beside Kevin Wilder on the settee. "Pardon me. I just have to sit."

Jonathan Pells shook his head and said to Scotty, "You won't believe it. She burned everything. My whole first draft, all my notes. In the barbecue pit."

"You're done. You're done!" Graves shouted. "I'll buy you for a dollar!" he taunted as he tried to break out of the circle that hemmed him in. Beside him, Cecilia Burnett simply stared. I'm going to be on television, after all, she thought. Imagine.

And then the double doors of Ballroom A opened once again and Eduardo Vinici entered. He closed the door with his body weight and slumped against it. "Help me," he gasped, and all the cameras swung to him. He slid down the door to the floor.

"Nobody touch him," Detective Scott ordered. He stooped in an attempt to aid the banquet manager.

"I locked him in the attic," Eduardo Vinici managed to say, his whole body shaking.

And in the stunned silence, while the cameras recorded events, Deirdre Day Tully cackled loud and long.

MR. V, AT HIS INSISTENCE, was helped to his office by Detective Scott and a stout houseman. He refused to have the hotel doctor summoned.

Mr. Enders, Hepplewhite's general manager, asked the writers to disperse to their rooms, thereby putting an end to the interviews. Several reporters elected to stay in the public bar to await developments. Others, with their technicians, returned to their respective stations. They would hear quickly enough if more news broke.

Scotty loosened Mr. V's expensive tie and perfectly fitting collar. Only his left hand was shaking now. "Of course I won't go to the hospital," he said with spirit when Scotty asked him yet again. "The murderer!" Mr. V was trying to explain. "It's the new man, Romeo. He went up to the thirty-fifth-floor storeroom. I trapped him there."

"But that's incredible," Scotty argued. "Why would this man of yours murder Muriel Lake?"

"These days there's no why or wherefore," Mr. V panted, white from shock, but rallying. And then, just like that, his palsy stopped. "These days the crazies just do things. Remember Hinckley? It's their fault," he rambled. "Mystery writers and those silly novels they write."

"What you need is whiskey," Scotty decided. "That'll bring your color back. I can see you've already found your nerve."

Someone from the kitchen staff quickly brought Mr. V a whiskey. He drank it right back and silently marveled at his steady left hand. "We must go after him," he said to Detective Scott. "The man won't wait up there for us to bring his noose. He'll break out. He'll get away. We must get him."

"You're in no shape for that," Scotty said.

"I insist!" Mr. V stood up. "Come, I'll take several kitchen men. You can make the arrest."

"I've got an officer here," Scotty said, referring to the policeman who had escorted Jonathan Pells to the Riverdale estate to look for Muriel Lake's manuscript. "Two of us should be enough. Any more and the whole hotel would empty, eh?"

"Horrors," Mr. V breathed, envisioning it. "That's right. This way we can keep it quiet. Let's go."

SIXTEEN

ROMEO POPOI HAD FOUND what he had come to the attic for, what he had dedicated his future to find: the personnel file of his father, Plato Popoi, discharged in April 1970 for theft.

According to the file, the elder Popoi had been suspected of sneaking foodstuffs out of the hotel for some time. A private detective was hired to watch him, he had been seen leaving through the delivery door in the basement with a box of frozen lobsters. The detective had followed him to the back entrance of a midtown seafood restaurant, where he had been photographed handing over the box to the chef in exchange for an envelope. He had been discharged the following day. There was no further notation, no added information that Plato Popoi, vehemently protesting his innocence, had left the Hepplewhite vowing vengeance. There was no mention of the fact that he had returned with a pistol and shot down the man who had fired him. But Romeo knew the man's name; his father had spoken of him often. That man had been Robert Alvopolis, and his file ended only with a single typed word: "deceased." There was no indication in any of the Hepplewhite files that a murder had ever taken place within the hotel.

"I was paid to take the boxes," Plato Popoi had told the court. "Every Wednesday, delivery day, after work, I was to go to that restaurant. It was a way this head man made extra money. Then an accountant discovered the food shortage, and I was made to take the rap. I was set up by the man who paid me to deliver the goods for him, the same man who fired me. I had to kill him. He was Greek. I was Greek. You cannot do such a thing to another man and live. I am innocent of theft, please believe, and I am innocent of murder. If was self-defense. It is our way. Ask any Greek. He would have done the same. We must, or we are not men...."

Plato Popoi had been found guilty. Romeo had been a baby in his mother's arms. When Romeo was old enough, he went to Ossining to visit his father, and Plato had charged him with clearing his name. His father wrote him regularly after that visit and then the letters stopped—Plato Popoi died six months before completing his sentence. Romeo had been fourteen then. He was twenty now, and he had wrestled with the charge given him for a long time. But he, too, was Greek, and a last command from one's father had to be obeyed. So Romeo had studied hard in high school and then worked in restaurants after class. Finally he went to a vocational school for hotel workers before joining the Hepplewhite.

He rummaged through the files, searching for something, anything that would prove the personnel man's treachery and his father's innocence. He doubted that he would find anything, and wondered what would become of him. He had hoped to search from time to time, undetected, until he found the thing that would prove Alvopolis's guilt and show the courts his father had been justified. But he'd found nothing; there was no accusation, and so how could there be vindication?

He was thirsty and afraid and wanted to leave. But he knew this was likely to be his only chance. If he could find the accountant's papers that showed the short count of the foodstuffs, and then the ones that Alvopolis made subtracting what he sold off for himself... But it was unlikely that Alvopolis had put anything on paper. Mr. V had seen him, and so he knew his job was over. He would join his father in shame and go to prison. Romeo was sorry for that. He liked the Hepplewhite and wanted to stay. But it had to be done, he consoled himself. He would continue to look until they dragged him away. His father, in his grave, deserved as much.

He heard footsteps on the stairs and knew they were coming. He riffled through the last papers in his hand. Nothing. The hotel didn't keep signed receipts for food deliveries from that long ago. And Robert Alvopolis of personnel had worked upstairs, cool in his shirt-sleeves, not in a burning kitchen. He had changed the number of boxes delivered and sold off the ones he was able to subtract. There was no record.

Romeo Popoi heard the key tumble the cylinders.

There was a little window where he was, in a dormer overlooking the roof. If he broke it, they might think he had escaped and they would leave the attic to continue their hunt elsewhere. What did he have to lose? he thought, and rushed the window with the drawer to a filing cabinet. The old glass shattered and he hurled the drawer through the hole. Romeo heard it hit the roof and bounce, heard the whip of pigeons' wings. Then he flattened himself behind a tall metal cabinet and prayed.

CECILIA BURNETT had been in her room for almost half an hour before she noticed the envelope. It was not like her; she was usually observant of her surroundings. But she was having trouble understanding all that was whirling around her.

Augustus Graves had been Muriel's lover! Cecilia's publisher had been the man who had stolen Muriel from Jonathan Pells. And he hadn't been ashamed of it; he had stepped up beside Cecilia and told the world. Astonishing. And then he had spoken to her, "Meet me tonight before dinner, my dear, in the piano lounge. I have things to say to you."

Cecilia was a little afraid to go. Not so afraid that she wouldn't, but she thought she didn't trust Augustus Graves anymore. He and Gordon Gates, with whom Cecilia for some reason felt more comfortable, had had such a terrible public fight in the ballroom. And then the poor banquet manager claimed he had trapped the murderer; who could it be? Was Muriel Lake's murderer really only a stranger? Was that how murder happened in real life, accidental, unmotivated? No, Cecilia thought, it couldn't be. Not this time....

And then, frustrated and indecisive, she finally saw the envelope, milky white, turned at an angle in the middle of her bed.

"Oh," she said out loud, and reached for it. It will be from Kevin, she thought, something clever, perhaps another clue.

But it wasn't from Kevin, and it was unsigned. She read it quickly, then slowly:

I hate you, too
What fell on one
can
fall
on two

DDT, she thought, and folded the letter back inside the envelope. Crazy old lady. She wrote hate letters to Muriel Lake and now she's picking on me. Well, I won't let her.

Beyond her door Cecilia could hear the varied laughter and voices of mystery writers having a party in the hall. She could hear their steps as they moved among each other and their thumps as they propped their bodies against the walls. She listened for DDT's particular laughter, that piercing bray, but didn't hear it. Cecilia sighed. She would have to go in search of the lady and tell her not to do this anymore. And Deirdre Day Tully had once been such a heroine to Cecilia; Cecilia had loved her books.

Before she left, Cecilia tucked her diary notebook under her pillow. Just to be safe, she thought.

And then she combed her hair, set the barrette straight and rubbed a little color on her cheeks and lips before opening her door. Everyone at the conference seemed to be milling in the hall.

"Have you seen DDT?" Cecilia asked Herman Patrick's plump friend, who was talking to three men Cecilia didn't know.

"Try JoAnn and Gilda's room," he said, and then he turned back to his three colleagues. "Herman turned over DDT's hate letters to Detective Scott before the press interview. She's his number one suspect after Jonathan."

Cecilia thanked him and moved away. She didn't know JoAnn and Gilda's room number, but she saw Stash Yarrow talking to Alice Ludlow and Jonathan and twisted through the crowd to ask him.

"Eleven o'clock tonight," he greeted her. "We'll all be on the news. Don't miss it."

Cecilia brightened. "I'm on Channel 2," she said. "I hope."

"We're going up to the thirty-fifth floor," Alice said. "They've trapped the murderer there and we've decided to get in on that."

"Can't bear not to," Gilda added, appearing in an open doorway, her low bodice now covered by a loose black sweater. "Want to come?"

Cecilia shook her head. "I've got to see DDT. What's her room number, Stash?"

"Four-seven-nine. Around the corner, down the hall." He pointed.

Cecilia had the letter in her hand. She wanted to tell the others about it, but didn't. They were heading for the elevator, excited, amused. She followed Stash Yarrow's directions and found the room quickly. "Ms Tully?" she called out as she knocked.

"Come in."

Cecilia tried the doorknob. It turned and she opened the door and stepped in. The room was identical to hers, although the color scheme was different. Instead of Cecilia's blue and cream, this room was pink and coral. Deirdre Day Tully sat in the chair before the window. Cecilia took a good look at the woman. Tiny wrinkles traced a web upon her face and her hair was thin and limp. Her ears looked extra large and her eyes seemed to be sinking into their sockets. At this distance it was clear that her heavy black dress was old and in need of repair. Why she's a bundle of rags, Cecilia thought. She can't be making much money. And after such wonderful books.

"DDT," Cecilia said as she moved across the room to sit on the older woman's bed. "Did you send me this letter?"

"And what if I did? You're getting much too big for your britches. Much too fast."

"No," Cecilia said. "No, I'm not, and you mustn't do these things. They don't become you."

"Becoming. What do you know of becoming?" The voice was hard and flat, not old. The voice held health and power. "I've become, I've been. You're the one who's becoming, and dearie, you've a lot yet to become."

Cecilia laid the letter on the bed and smoothed it with her hand. "This letter sounds like a threat. I've never done anything to you. And it almost sounds as if you killed Muriel, which I know you didn't."

"I know who killed her," Deirdre Day Tully said, and she cackled.

"They say they've caught the killer on a high floor of the hotel, right now, this very minute."

"Ha," the older woman answered, and she smiled a little.

Cecilia tore the envelope's blank face, and the paper gaped in her hands. "What have I done to make you hate me?" She placed the two ripped pieces side by side, fitting their torn pieces together.

The older woman shifted in the chair. "Oh, get out. I can't bear to look at you." Her arm jumped in the air to indicate the door.

"I've admired you all my life," Cecilia said. "Don't do this."

DDT's chin lifted. "Your new champion, your Augustus Graves? Well, he used to be mine. And now, guess what?"

"What?"

"He told me today that my new book won't do. Yours will, he said. Your book is good. *Slumber Said the Sandman* is going to be a big book on his fall list. Well, I say it won't."

"Oh, DDT. That's not my book. Mine's *Death Wakes Up*, and they'll probably print five thousand copies like the first one and sell them to the libraries. You have nothing to be jealous about."

The older writer sat up. Her chin was still lifted proudly. "Quit playing the innocent. You mean you don't know?"

"Don't know what?" Cecilia's heart was beating faster, pushing in her chest. She put a hand on her breast to hold it steady. "Don't know what?"

DDT laughed meanly. "He's renamed it, you little fool. You're top of the list."

Cecilia couldn't take it in. "Renamed *Death Wakes Up*?"

"Oh, shut up! Yes, you dim child. Augustus Graves has turned down the latest Deirdre Day Tully and taken a child's effort and is wrapping it in gold. Well, he won't get away with it, because I know. I saw him last night coming out of the library. I saw him, I let him go, I went in behind. And Muriel was dead, hot and flowing-blood dead, just killed. You won't have your big book, dearie, because your publisher's going to jail. I'll have my pound of flesh. He won't throw me aside and get away with—''

Cecilia ran.

Somewhere upstairs, high in that vast building, Detective Scott was capturing Augustus Graves. She couldn't believe it. Mr. Graves had been with her when the banquet manager had staggered in.

She found a bank of elevators and waited, trembling, rubbing her hands together. DDT was mad. It couldn't be so!

A door opened behind her. "Wait for me!" Deirdre Day Tully called.

And then it was Cecilia's turn to laugh. "Yes," she said. "But hurry."

SEVENTEEN

DETECTIVE SCOTT DIDN'T carry a gun. He stood at the door of the long, low room, its ceiling tilted at different angles to accommodate the varying lines of the hotel roof, and considered the situation. Mr. V snapped on the overhead lights; bare bulbs blazed in a circle around the room.

There were rows of filing cabinets, some gray, others green, stacks of boxes and an assortment of broken tables and worn folding chairs. Several cots and a few old hotel lamps sat against one wall. The space was a storage room, hot. But now, so high over the city, a strong draught blew from the broken window. On the ledge a pigeon looked at Scotty and swayed its purple neck.

Scotty took a few steps into the room, gestured to the others to hold back and looked around. The pigeon flew. The light from the bare bulbs threw little shadow. The walls behind him were lined with filing cabinets. Ahead there was dust and a line of smudged footprints. Scotty followed the line to the farthest portion of the room, near the open window, where there was a fortress of filing cabinets.

He's either on the roof or hiding in there, the detective thought. Perhaps he has a gun.

"Come out now," Scotty called. "It's all over. Come out and you won't be hurt." He waited, expecting nothing. "Tyrrell, check outside. Take Mr. V's man with you."

"Yes, sir."

The police officer and the houseman advanced through the dust to the window. The policeman knocked out the bits of jagged glass still hanging to the window frame with his handgun and then cautiously climbed through the window. The other man quickly followed him.

Then Scotty heard something, a soft sound, like a foot slipping on loose paper. It came from the direction of the filing cabinets across the room.

"All right, come out," he said, putting no emotion into his voice. "Don't make it worse for yourself."

He thought he could see a shadow, hunched, tense.

Beside him, the exasperated voice of Mr. V pleaded, "Come out and tell us what the problem is. Perhaps we can work it out. Really!"

And then a clear voice responded, "My father was Plato Popoi. I want his records, that's all."

Mr. V stepped in front of Scotty. His left hand was now strong and steady. "I've never heard of your father, man. Come out. Talk to us."

And again the voice came from behind the files near the window. "He killed a man who worked here and went to prison unjustly. I want to clear his name."

The banquet manager turned to the detective. "I can handle this," he said softly. "All right, Romeo, let's talk about it. Just come out, please."

"Don't fire me, sir. I'll help you. I'll work at the hotel twenty-four hours a day."

"Come out and stop this nonsense immediately. God, I've had enough trouble today. We shall have to work all night setting things right."

"Yes sir. Send the others away?" It was the voice of a scared child.

"No," Mr. V responded. "Be a man, Romeo, and come out. We'll go down to my office and have a talk. A short talk—there's work to be done."

Finally Romeo emerged from his hiding spot. He stood, dust in his hair, yellow papers in his hand, fear and challenge in his stance before the men. "Don't betray me," he pleaded.

Mr. V turned to Scotty. "Call in the men and let's get out of here. I'll handle Romeo. He needs attention, not handcuffs."

Scotty nodded, relieved the crisis had proven so small. "Well done," he said. He had things to do, too, bigger things, harder things. "Tyrrell, come in. Game's over," he called.

Mr. V walked to the empty space in the middle of the room. Shuffling, Romeo came out. Mr. V clapped a hand on the young man's shoulder. "There's a right way and a wrong way, Romeo," he began.

"Yes, sir."

Scotty and the others left the room, followed by Mr. V and Romeo. Mr. V stopped to turn the key, pull it out and then place it into his pocket. "And now the master, Romeo. Please give it to me."

Romeo handed him the key but kept his head down, looking at no one.

There were people and voices in the hallway of the thirty-fourth floor. Mr. V saw a half-dozen mystery writers and felt his fury rise. "Please, get rid of them," he said to Detective Scott. "Take them down the far elevator. Romeo and I will use my private lift."

Scotty nodded. He and Tyrrell went forward. "It was all a mistake," Scotty said. "We must go back down. This involves a different murder entirely."

"Then Muriel *was* murdered?" Deirdre Day Tully demanded.

Scotty didn't answer.

"Oh, God, what a fine hotel this is," Stanislas Yarrow said, and the writers laughed and cheered.

"Do you hear, Romeo, what a grand hotel this is?" Mr. V led the young man to the private elevator.

"It is the most wonderful hotel," Romeo agreed, "and I want to work here forever."

"I'll make you my assistant," Mr. V said. "I'll teach you everything I know. That will clear your father's name. That will be his legacy."

"And in gratitude I'll solve your murder for you, Mr. V."

"Oh, Romeo, it's not my murder. Detective Scott is very qualified. Stay out of that mess. Promise me."

They were in the elevator, going down slowly.

"But I found the murder weapon," Romeo said. "In the library. I showed it to the husband. He was grateful."

Mr. V sighed and smoothed his gray hair with a steady left hand. He looked at the two of them, old and young, in the high, round elevator mirror. "All right. We'll see the detective again, Romeo, after we talk, in the lull before dinner. You'll tell him everything you know of the murder of Muriel Lake."

EIGHTEEN

DETECTIVE SCOTT FOUND Augustus Graves in the piano lounge of the Gardenia Room by accident. He went there for a drink, to have some time alone to think. The piano player began at nine, so the stools around the black baby grand were empty, and the keyboard cover down. But Jonathan Pells and Alice Ludlow were sitting on the piano bench, their two glasses resting on paper napkins on either side of the sheet music stand. They were holding hands and staring morosely at another couple in a corner booth. The woman was the pale young writer who had come to Scotty's room. She was sitting with Augustus Graves.

Scotty looked away, not wanting company. He didn't want to talk to Jonathan—that friendship was over. He didn't want to continue working on the investigation of the death of Muriel Lake, but he didn't know how to withdraw. He just wanted to sit in this dark, cold room, undisturbed, and drink.

"Double Scotch on the rocks," he said to the waitress, a pretty blonde.

But Augustus Graves saw him, rose a little from his corner booth and vigorously gestured for the detective to come over.

Sighing to himself, Scotty went.

"Have a drink, Detective Scott. I must tell you my story." The woman made a gesture, as though to excuse herself. Graves stopped her by resting a finger on her arm. "No, no, my dear, you listen. It'll do you good. You're going to be the next Muriel Lake, so think of this as a cautionary tale."

Cecilia Burnett sat back down. Her face was flushed, which gave it color, and Scotty admired again her delicate beauty.

The waitress brought Scotty's drink, the large man indicated that the charge should be added to his tab, and then the publisher began his story. "I met Muriel Lake last year. I was courting her to come back to Tombstone. We met a few times for lunches in the usual business way and found we liked each other. I've been single a long time, never really paid much attention to a private life—that's what ended my first marriage. But a man comes to a point in his life when he looks around and finds it empty. The business was running smoothly, nothing really challenging was happening, and I realized I was a rich man in my early sixties with nothing much ahead of me except time to enjoy the fruits of my labor. But I had no idea how to do that. I was ripe for love, you might say, and Muriel was, too."

"Sir," Cecilia said, "are you sure...?"

Graves patted her arm paternally. "I'm not embarrassed, Miss Burnett. I particularly want you to understand my relationship and last moments with Muriel. It will be good for both of us.''

Cecilia was quiet then, but her color increased and her green eyes glowed in the low-lit room. She sipped at the straw of her tall, frosted drink and avoided the detective's eyes.

"So," the publisher continued. "Muriel and I began a secret romance. We had a great deal of fun being secret and we fell in love. I talked her into reneging on her contract with Haunting House Press. Don't worry about the lawsuit, I said. I'll handle it. You're worth it. To be frank, I didn't think Haunting House could afford another expensive litigation, and I figured I'd kill two birds with one stone—steal Haunting House's best author, tie them up in court for a couple of seasons, and then buy them for pennies.''

"Not very nice," Scotty said, watching the woman. She wasn't wincing at the corporate piracy. She was listening intently as though she meant to use what she was hearing in a book.

"No," Graves conceded, "not very nice, but that's the way to play. So Muriel worked on the book and tried to help her husband get back on his feet and start a book of his own. She told me that was working out, that Jonathan still hit the bottle from time to time, but he was writing again and writing well. He had helped her with her manuscript—she freely admitted that— and he was working on a very good book of his own. She felt she could leave him and not feel guilty. She'd give him a generous settlement, enough to give him a good start, and he'd be all right.

"She was more concerned about Gordon Graves and breaking her contract. She felt Graves had been responsible, in part, for her success. She'd had her first big seller with him. He'd really gotten behind *The Blonde Was All in Red* and promoted the hell out of it. Well, it was his only chance. He was belly-up about that time, but I didn't harp on that. I promised her that Graves would get his million, a quarter of which he'd paid out to her, in full. I'd buy out Muriel's contract and he'd make seven hundred and fifty thousand dollars as a going-away present—if he didn't stand in our way. It all made sense—there are other writers out there, and it wouldn't be right for the wife of Augustus Graves to be published by the likes of Gordon Gates. Needless to say, I didn't tell her I meant to own Gates before I was through. Muriel wouldn't have liked that."

"No," Scotty agreed, remembering the Muriel he knew. During the time he had been falling in love with her then, she had belonged to this man. Not to Jonathan, not to him. She'd sold to the highest bidder, followed money and its sweet, sweet smell. Well, he'd known that about her. She hadn't hidden that. A person couldn't hide that; it showed, like sweat. Or maybe, Scotty mused, Muriel had really loved this guy—he was her kind of man. Scotty glanced again at Cecilia and wondered if she would meet Augustus Graves in a room tonight and unveil that slight white body so that Augustus Graves could cloak it in celebrity, just a little celebrity.... "We're all whores," Scotty said, and was surprised he'd spoken his thought out loud.

"Not Muriel," Augustus Graves defended. "She was no whore. She loved me."

And Scotty saw in the shrewd dark eyes of the publisher that he had indeed loved; that he was, indeed, hurting, mourning. So leave it alone, Scotty told himself. But at the same time he knew that men had killed for love. Did he find her with another lover? Is that what he's going to say?

Scotty dropped a finger into his glass and stirred the ice cubes. As if on cue, the waitress placed a second glass of Scotch before him. The blonde served the publisher another gin on ice, and Cecilia Burnett a concoction to match the first she had ordered and barely touched. Scotty watched Cecilia's reaction. She reached with plump lips to engulf the old straw and stretched out pale hands to pull the first glass closer. Her eyes followed movements on the far side of the room. Scotty turned and saw Jonathan, staring back from his seat on the piano bench.

Scotty turned back. "Go on," he said, because the publisher had stopped while the waitress served them.

Graves nodded, waved the waitress away and pulled out a pack of cigarettes. He placed them on the table, shook one out, set a gold-striped silver lighter beside it and pushed cigarette and lighter to the middle of the table under a copper-based lamp. "Five a day," Graves said. "I count them."

"Muriel," Scotty prompted.

Cecilia shifted in her seat and sipped her drink.

"Here's what happened," Graves continued. "The manuscript was finished. Muriel claimed she was afraid Jonathan would try to steal it. He had helped her a little and wanted co-credit. She said no. So before she left for the conference, she cut up the diskette, wiped the files off her hard disk, burned all the notes and hand-carried the only surviving copy to the hotel to hand over to me. I agreed with this policy. No second copies, no leaks, no problems. Once I had it in house we'd copy it and I'd keep the copies locked away.

"Okay. I was supposed to come Monday night, very late, after she'd checked in here. I was to meet her in Ballroom A and pick up *Unforgivable Sin*. But I didn't get over here until 8:00 a.m. Tuesday, maybe a little after. I stayed at the office and fell asleep. When I woke up at about six-thirty, I called her, went to her suite and took away the manuscript in a hurry. I didn't linger. I didn't want to be seen by any early arrivals to the convention and Pells was due in shortly. I didn't know Muriel was going to announce her imminent divorce the way she did. I had no part in that. I stayed home all day and night Tuesday, reading the five hundred pages."

He drooped a little, his shoulders tired of their burden. "I was to call her when I'd finished, tell her what

I thought. I wasn't due at the conference until today, Wednesday." He still hadn't lighted the cigarette. It rolled under his fingers, white on a white tablecloth. When he spoke again, his voice was duller, older. "I read the manuscript over and over. I couldn't believe what I was reading." He threw back his wild, white-maned hair and looked at Cecilia. "The manuscript was dreck," he said.

Cecilia jumped as though burned. "Bad?" she said, startled, uncomprehending.

"Dreadful. I thought I must be tired or having a breakdown or God knows what. But I know a good read from a bad one. I know a commercial book from a literary masterpiece. I know what will appeal, what will sell and what won't. This book was stale. Dull. No talent." The cigarette broke under his fingers. Tiny brown flecks danced across the table toward Scotty.

"Ohh." It was Cecilia, expelling breath.

Graves flicked the halves of cigarette away and dusted off his hands. "*Unforgivable Sin* is a piece of junk. Well—" his voice picked up vigor again "—I had a decision to make. Look, I loved the woman. Everyone's entitled to a weak effort once in a while, I thought. She's worn out with worry. The manuscript couldn't be fixed, but here's what we could do. Let Haunting House have it. Let her contract stand. She'd divorce Jonathan, we'd take a long honeymoon, the book would come out, and good luck to it. And Muriel would rejuvenate. She'd freshen. Then, after we were back, she'd do a new book for me. I'd watch her, keep her on track, and it would be all right. If I played my cards right, she'd never have to know what I thought of *Unforgivable Sin*. I'd just tell her I'd had a change of heart. Let the reviewers tell her, I thought, not me. No, I'd say I'd decided that we were going to start clean. Adam and Eve. We wouldn't eat that apple. We'd not cheat Gates. We'd be Mr. and Mrs. Ivory Pure. Okay.''

Without knowing it, Scotty had finished his second double and Cecilia Burnett was into her second frothy Collins. Scotty turned and saw that Jonathan and Alice were still there, behind them like specters, and that Jonathan was still watching them closely.

''And then?''

It was barely murmured, but Graves heard him. The publisher shook out another cigarette, and this time lighted it. ''And then I went to her,'' he said. ''I called her and asked to meet somewhere privately. I had new plans, exciting things to say. I had to see her. She said midnight, in the library here, Ballroom A. It would be closed, but she had an extra key, so I went.''

''Last night,'' Scotty said. You're not going to confess, you walrus, are you? he wondered.

''And so I came, a little after midnight, slipping in through the bar rather than the lobby so as not to attract attention. I went where she told me to go, opened the door, which was unlocked, and found her, as you did, so beautiful, so tragic. It must have only just happened. Her wrist was warm when I tried to find a pulse. The blood in her hair was still vibrant. It hadn't congealed. I opened her eyes to make sure—I want to forget the look in those glorious big-pupiled eyes.''

"They were dilated all the way?"

The publisher lifted his shoulders, then dropped them. "I suppose. They were huge and fixed. Please, let me go on."

"I'm sorry," Scotty said. "I just thought, perhaps—"

"No, man, she was dead. I'm sure of it. You don't think I'd leave her with a breath of life in her, do you?"

Scotty made a movement of his hand for the publisher to continue.

Graves was gruff now, irritable. "That's all. I ran, my tail between my legs. This morning I walked in and pretended not to know what had happened. I panicked, I'm ashamed to say. I should have woken up the whole hotel last night, called an ambulance, told my story immediately. But she was so dead who had been more alive than anyone else I'd ever known. All our plans, our dreams, we were on the threshold. Well, it shook me. I was lost. It took me all day to get up the courage to approach you—" he lifted his glass "—and maybe a few stiff drinks. I've seen Gates, turned the manuscript over to him, said nothing about its quality, of course. I apologized, told him Muriel just gave it over to me for safekeeping, and as far as I know, that's that. He's got Muriel Lake's last book. Even if it does stink, it'll sell like crack now that she's gone." He drew deeply on his cigarette.

Scotty drained the last of his glass, ice water now. "What time did you say you left her?"

Cecilia started to speak, then stopped.

"Maybe twenty after midnight," Graves answered. "When I saw that she was dead, I didn't stay long. God forgive me."

Scotty pushed his chair back. "Is there anything else?"

The publisher shook his head. "Nothing more I can think of. If you have any questions, I'm staying here for the rest of the week. Room 503. Under the circumstances, I want to be here. I want, more than most, to know what happened to her."

"Sure," Scotty said. "Under the circumstances, of course, you would. Room 503, right?"

"Deirdre Day Tully saw you, Mr. Graves," Cecilia said. "She said she saw you coming out of the ballroom and called to you, but you didn't stop, so she went in to see what was going on."

Graves stiffened. "Oh, DDT, yes. I did see her and managed to avoid her, scooting out the way I was." He shook his head and the gray hair floated. "She's a little crazy, I think. When writers run dry, or stay past their time... Went in where?"

"To the library," Cecilia said. "So she says."

"She's making that up," he said, and crushed out his cigarette. "She's a liar. She's desperate. What exactly did she say?"

"She hasn't spoken to me," Scotty said, and he waited, too, to hear.

"She said that when she went into the room, Miss Lake was dead. And if she told me, she'll tell others. She's angry, Mr. Graves."

The big man nodded. "She would be."

Scotty had been half out of his chair, but he sank down again.

"Well." Cecilia sipped at her second drink. The straw made a gulping noise; the drink was finished now. She looked from one to the other.

"Go on. Out with it." There was an edge in Graves's voice.

Cecilia nodded and took a deep breath. "She says you turned down her new book."

"Yes," the publisher acknowledged, "I did. She should let it go. She used to be good. She's got enough money to live on. She doesn't need to write. But she doesn't want to leave the party. It's over for her, but don't feel bad. Someday it's over for all of us. She had a good run."

Cecilia nodded. "Yes, I'm learning that, Mr. Graves."

"Make hay while the sun shines, Cecilia," he said. "After every harvest comes a winter."

She looked at Scotty in that solemn way he'd seen before, as though she wanted comfort.

Graves signaled for the bill. "You're in your salad days, young lady. You'll have a great career if you can keep up the good work. Write while you can. That's my best advice to any writer. And remember, nothing lasts forever."

"I'll excuse myself now if you don't mind," Cecilia said. "It's almost dinnertime. I ought to dress."

"We'll sit together at dinner," Graves said. "Wear something glamorous. It's time you learned how."

"Ohh," she said, and left, fading into the dark walls and leather of the room. Both men watched her go. She stopped beside Jonathan and Alice and said something, then walked on, not looking back.

"Cute kid," Scotty said.

"Not a kid, my friend," the publisher argued, signing his name to the bill. "There goes a fine and subtle intelligence, and a dream of a mystery writer. She's going to be very big."

"That's what they said of Muriel," Scotty returned.

"Used to say," Graves corrected.

"Used to say, yes."

The way out led past the piano bench. Scotty acknowledged Jonathan and wanted to keep going, but Pells spoke to him.

"I keep expecting Mu to walk in," Jonathan said, and his smile twisted. "Don't you?"

NINETEEN

DINNER THAT EVENING was subdued; there was little of the laughter and lightness of earlier that afternoon. Two reporters had been invited to stay on to listen to Dr. Fu Song's explanation of the murder. They sat at a table with the forensic pathologist and Detective Scott and they weren't bothered by writers. The novelists seemed to realize that they'd had their individual media moments, and now they grouped together to represent a public image of WOM, their writers' organization.

Gordon Gates, however straight-faced and correct in his black suit, seemed to be the only one in the room hard-pressed to keep from smiling. He had, at last, *Unforgivable Sin* in its pretty blue box. He'd already had it copied twice by the hotel. He'd given one copy to Alice, kept one for himself and had triumphantly sent the original—by messenger—to the Haunting House offices. He hadn't had the time to read the manuscript yet, but he was content. Masterpiece or not, the novel would succeed. With Muriel's dramatic death and the publicity campaign he would mount capitalizing upon it, success was a fait accompli. And if the manuscript was weak, although Muriel had claimed it was her best by far, he would fix it, Alice would fix it. Everything was going to turn out all right, after all—Haunting House's fortunes were assured. He felt better, too, about Augustus Graves. "Damn decent of Graves to turn *Sin* over," he'd said to Alice Ludlow when he presented her with a copy, "even though he took his sweet time about it."

"Yes," she'd agreed. "And I think under the circumstances that you should be decent, too, and publish Jonathan's next book. After all, how could you gain by her death and not help her widower? I plan to marry Jon, and my position is simple, Gordon—take him or lose me. I have a standing offer to join Tombstone."

He'd capitulated. "All right, all right," he'd said, spreading his hands. "See how magnanimous I am. I'll take Jonathan back. All's well that ends well, eh?"

"Except there's a murderer among us."

Now, at the table with Jonathan and Alice, Gordon Gates tried to keep his smiles to himself as he ate his duck with gusto. Herman Patrick and his plump friend sat at Gordon's table, too, but they were both quiet. Deirdre Day Tully took the sixth chair.

"I have a manuscript for you, Gordon," DDT said as she sat down. "Are you interested?" She looked older than he'd ever seen her; the usual gleam in her eyes was gone.

"I'd be interested in seeing anything by the first lady of crime," he began gallantly, "but, Deirdre, I've never published you. Hasn't Graves renewed your contract?'' Deirdre Day Tully's best work had been years ago—and everybody knew it.

He was surprised to see her flinch. "It's called *Hate Letters*," the older writer said. "Augustus Graves is begging to see it, but I need a change."

Gordon Gates understood: Tombstone had rejected it and DDT needed to sell her book. Well, I won't worry about it now, he thought. If the new one's like her last four or five, I'll pass, too. I'll let Alice handle it.

"You're an expert on hate letters," Herman Patrick said abruptly, and his plump friend tittered.

"Oh," DDT said as she sliced the duck. "Has little Cecilia Burnett been talking?"

"I was referring to Muriel," Herman corrected. "Have you been bothering our newest member and volunteer recording secretary, the diligent Cecilia? Shame on you, DDT. Why don't you pick on someone your own size? She's just starting out in our business."

"Cecilia Burnett says I did. She's lying, of course." The grande dame laughed, but the laughter was forced and lacked fire.

"Muriel sent me some of your fan letters," Herman continued. "Remember now?"

"She was mean to me," Deirdre Day Tully argued. "I just let her know she couldn't get away with it."

"And she didn't, did she?" Jonathan said, something raging behind his eyes.

"Yes, very incriminating, DDT," Alice added. "Did you meet Muriel in the library Tuesday night? Was it you, after all? Everyone's saying it was."

"I—"

Jonathan Pells looked DDT in the eye. "You'll get yours. Just wait."

DDT tried to rally. "Old age breeds desperation," she said, chewing duck. "And so does not being able to sell your latest book. You should know about that, Jonathan, and you weren't an angel to Muriel, either."

Alice put her hand on Jonathan's knee to calm him. Herman Patrick and his friend bent silently over their plates. Gordon Gates inwardly smiled; nothing could blot this day for him. Let DDT and Pells go at each other, *kill each other*. He disliked them both.

"Gingham dog and calico cat," Gordon said to a silent table. "Both ate each other, and that was that."

CECILIA BURNETT SAT with Augustus Graves, Kevin Wilder, JoAnn Morris, Gilda Shapiro and Stanislas Yarrow a few tables over from Gordon Gates and his entourage.

JoAnn and Gilda were wearing matching black gowns with black ribbons around their necks. Cecilia, trying to fulfill her publisher's expectations of her, wore JoAnn Morris's leopard print dress. It became her, but she was uncomfortable in it. Her red hair hung loose around her shoulders, her cheeks and lips had been rouged, her green eyes emphasized with mascara. Suddenly she was beautiful, and she didn't know how to carry it. She told the table about DDT's hate letter.

"She's a sad old lady," Kevin, sitting on Cecilia's left, said. "Forget her. Just be nice and let it go. In her day she was a good writer. That's the way to remember her."

"DDT's a monster," Gilda said. "Always was, always will be. Even when she was in her prime. It wasn't enough for her to succeed. She wanted everyone else to fail. And when Muriel began to climb, DDT really hated her. She thought Muriel dethroned her on purpose. Crazy DDT. She's the only one of us I can believe killed Muriel. She's the only one mean enough."

"Or bold enough," JoAnn added. "DDT's a good plotter. If it was murder, I think she did it."

"Horsefeathers," Stash disagreed. "Muriel killed herself. A purposeful suicide, when I threw her over for you, my dear." And he looked teasingly at Gilda Shapiro, who pantomimed laughter at him.

"That would be impossible," Kevin said, and everyone at the table looked at him politely. He wasn't one of them, not yet a professional. Cecilia knew they didn't mind his presence if he were seen and not heard, but they resented his participation.

"Kevin has just finished his first book, Mr. Graves," she said, and Kevin looked at her with true love.

"That right, young man?" the publisher boomed, and he stretched forward to look at Kevin more closely.

"Yes, sir," Kevin confirmed. "But I won't show it to anybody until Ceci here reads it. If she says it's okay, I'll send it to you."

"Well, she'd know. Cecilia Burnett's my shining new star. You like her, do you?"

"She's all right, sir," Kevin said, embarrassed. "We just met here at the conference."

"Tell them your theory about Muriel," Cecilia prompted him.

"Let's wait to hear what Dr. Song tells us," he said.

"Well, I've solved it," Stash announced. "It was Gordon Gates. He needed a big news hook for Muriel's new book, and now he's got one. You've got to look at who benefits."

"Oh," Gilda interrupted. "I think Ceci's right. It was Muriel's lover. Stash Yarrow, stand up and confess."

"Muriel's lover was Augustus Graves," Cecilia corrected unthinkingly. "Please, Gilda."

"And Stash Yarrow," Kevin said, pointing his fork at the thriller writer. "I mean, before Mr. Graves."

"And who knows who else," Augustus Graves added. "Muriel was a lusty woman. Now let's leave it, shall we?"

And their table, too, lapsed into an uneasy silence.

And then the dinner was over and Dr. Song stood up to speak. He was a small man, neat in a blue pinstripe suit. He adjusted the microphone clipped to his lapel before looking out at his audience.

"Yes, my good friends," the doctor began, "your worst suspicions are confirmed. The death of Muriel Lake was no accident. She was murdered by design. Murdered, I might add, by someone with a macabre sense of humor."

The room buzzed, then fell silent. Only Deirdre Day Tully, cracking the lid of her chocolate coffin-shaped dessert, made any noise.

"On or about Tuesday night, just after midnight, in the room adjoining us here to the right, Muriel Lake was bludgeoned to death. The instrument used was a heavy, flat-sided object, a portable safe, weighing some thirty-plus pounds, so constructed to look like a dictionary. This is a photograph of the murder weapon." He lifted a black-and-white eight-by-ten picture. "I'll start it around the room with this table." He handed the photo to the news reporters.

Again the room buzzed. Most of them hadn't known about the safe.

Dr. Song waited for the writers' attention before continuing. "The murder object was discovered by Jonathan Pells, Miss Lake's husband, and turned over to me for investigation purposes."

Heads swiveled toward Jonathan.

"Of course it was easy for him to find," Deirdre Day Tully sniped, and her voice carried across the room. Under cover of the table, Alice Ludlow took Jonathan's hand and held it tightly.

"Miss Lake was struck twice," Dr. Song continued. "The first time was from behind, and I think she was sitting, or kneeling perhaps, on the floor, because the blow landed with unusual force as though swung from arm's length. It's likely that the safe was grasped in both hands in an overhand swat. This first blow hit the back of her head and broke through the skull, undoubtedly causing unconsciousness but not her death."

The doctor waited for the room to absorb this news. The reporters had a tape recorder on and were taking notes. Cecilia Burnett also took notes. Augustus Graves sat with his hands folded in his lap, his eyes closed. Jonathan Pells stared down at his uneaten dessert. A single tear trickled down his cheek.

"She must have fallen to the left," the controlled voice of the doctor continued. "She bled profusely from the crown of her head. Happily feeling nothing, I'm certain. Her new position made the right side of her face vulnerable, and that's where the murderer struck next. Again, a swung blow, but shorter the second time. Perhaps he knelt above her to see what damage he had caused. I use 'he' in the general sense. There's no reason the force of the blows couldn't have been delivered by a female. It was more the weight of the murder tool than the strength of the murderer that inflicted the mortal wounds, although of course some strength in the arms and shoulders would be necessary. It was the second blow that killed her. A corner of the safe broke through Miss Lake's right temple and pierced the brain, fatally traumatizing about two-fifths of it. Death followed within moments, say ninety seconds after the second attack.''

The room was completely quiet.

''Now. Miss Lake had a book in her hands at the time, a copy of what I'm told was her first success, the mystery novel *The Blonde Was All in Red*. When she fell from the first blow, the fingers of her left hand still held that book by its bottom. The book was opened, its front cover turned back. And in Miss Lake's right hand, found tucked against her stomach, was a gold Tiffany rollerball pen, its point turned in position to write.'' The doctor held up a sealed plastic bag that held the pen, its point visibly extracted.

''And on the inside of the opened front cover there's a pen mark, a long slash.'' Dr. Song reached down into a satchel he had placed on his chair and pulled out another plastic bag. It contained the book with its front cover open and one long black figure clearly visible. There was a short backward cap to it and a long straight line descending. The doctor laid book and pen on the table. ''I cannot pass these evidential items around, ladies and gentlemen, but after my talk any or all of you may come up to look at them. Please do not touch.''

The room was as silent as a tomb. No one raised a glass, or rattled ice, or exhaled upon his cigarette. And then Deirdre Day Tully crashed into the silence again. ''She was autographing her book,'' she shouted.

Dr. Song nodded, unperturbed at the old woman's bad manners. "Yes," he said, "I think you may be right. But that's the second part of my explanation. That's supposition. I want to finish with the direct evidence first, what you mystery writers like to call 'the facts,' yes?"

"Yes," Deirdre Day Tully barked before slurping from her coffee cup.

"The mark looks to my staff and myself," Dr. Song said, ignoring DDT's confirmation, "like the beginning of a capital letter. An *F*, *B*, *H*. It might be an *I*, or *K*, *M*, *N*, *P*, *R*, *W*, and I allow a possible *Z*. To try to discover which, we consulted with Mr. Pells today and he brought us several examples of Miss Lake's handwriting, and several books that she had autographed to him."

Again heads turned Jonathan's way. He was sitting two seats away from Deirdre Day Tully. Gordon Gates and Alice Ludlow separated him from her. But Jonathan gave no sign that he was aware of DDT's disrespectful performance. He had removed the tear from his cheek, or it had dried on its own. He was sitting with his head alert, his eyes on the doctor. Alice Ludlow's hand still rested in his own on his lap.

"In examining the book notations," Dr. Song began, "we discovered Miss Lake habitually began her autographing with a 'for.' So we have, as one of you has already brightly remarked, tentatively identified the pen mark as the beginning of an *F*. There's no crossbar, so I hasten to add we're not certain, but the slash is like her *F*'s. So I suggest that Miss Lake was crouching or kneeling on the rug of Ballroom A, before the bookcase, in the presence of a person or persons she knew enough to be at ease with, but not so well that an autographed copy of her book wouldn't be an appropriate gift. She opened the book's cover, turned it back flat to write, inclined her head . . . and met her doom."

The doctor paused to sip from his water glass, then pressed on. "Then the murderer wiped the dictionary-safe clean. If he or she opened the safe, they chose to ignore the contract drawn up between Miss Lake and Haunting House Press for a book tentatively titled *Unforgivable Sin*. There might, of course, have been something else in the safe that was removed, but that again is speculation. The murderer wiped the weapon clean and dropped it beside his victim. Then he, I think at this time, put on gloves or used a table napkin or handkerchief and pulled the books from the bookcase or actually threw them at the body. There were no prints on the books. Many of the books are bent at the corners and top and bottom of the spine. And then—I'm almost done and then I'll take questions—and then the murderer moved the bookcase out from the wall, got behind and toppled it on the unfortunate woman's body. There was a crash. At least one member of your organization heard it, I'm told, and the villain ran. He might have left by the inner doors that lead from that room into this, or by the doors of Ballroom A, quickly, boldly. He might have been seen, although it seems he wasn't."

"Oh, yes, he was," Deirdre Day Tully screamed, and she pushed herself up from her chair and pointed at Augustus Graves. "And there he is. I saw him myself, sneaking out and down the hall to the bar and then to the street." Gordon Gates pulled DDT down. She fought furiously, trying to rise again. "But it's true! It's true!" she yelled.

"Shut up, you old fool," Gates spit at her.

And she subsided, shifting her eyes to Jonathan. "You pansy," she said. "How can you just sit there?"

Alice stood and pulled Jonathan up with her. They moved to another table, where there was no one, and sat close together, dignified and proud.

Dr. Song used the time to drink from his glass again. A waiter brought him a fresh one. The writers in the room shifted, too. Some began to finish their clever desserts, while others pushed their chairs back and crossed their legs.

Herman Patrick raised his hand.

"Yes," Dr. Song said, "I'll take questions now. Sir?"

"Have you ascertained any motive, Doctor?" Patrick asked, then sat back down.

Dr. Song shook his head. "That's not my province. That's Detective Scott's department. Scotty?"

Scotty stayed as he was, sitting, and shook his head.

Patrick's plump friend was recognized next. "Are we all still under suspicion?"

Scotty stood this time. "I'm sorry to have kept such a close rein on you all. Simply advise one of my officers where you can be reached if you decide to leave the hotel. We may have further questions to ask some of you."

"Who's your prime suspect, Detective Scott?" someone called out.

"I'm not prepared to say," Scotty said with a smile.

"Augustus Graves!" Deirdre Day Tully shouted.

"I say you," someone else screamed at DDT.

"All right, all right, that's the end of this entertainment," Scotty announced. And the writers stood and applauded the doctor, who unpinned his microphone, returned it to a reporter and began quickly repacking his bag.

Scotty moved to join the doctor, and writers surged forward to ask private questions of their own.

No one paid any attention to DDT, who suddenly slumped in her chair as though weary and laid her head on the table. Her face was in her chocolate coffin.

TWENTY

2:00 a.m., Thursday, May 12

CECILIA BURNETT BEGAN writing in her diary.

We were all so exhausted that everyone said quick good-nights and departed for his or her room. I hung back for a few moments to visit the doctor's table to look at the pen and book and the picture of the safe that had never gotten around to us. The pen gave me chills because it was the one Miss Lake had used to autograph her book to me, which now has an importance in my library far beyond just a personalized copy from a friend. Detective Scott asked me if Kevin and I had solved the mystery yet. I said I had eliminated Augustus Graves and Jonathan Pells. He said one of them was therefore sure to be the guilty party, or at least that was the way it often worked.

Two waiters helped DDT off to her room. She was stumbling as though drunk and she cursed them all on the way out. I, worn out, came back to my room, where I carefully got out of JoAnn's leopard dress, ironed it and hung it in the little closet to go back to her tomorrow.

Then I showered, slipped into my nightdress and climbed into bed to write in my diary just as the clock in the library below me began to chime again. It was very spooky, a replay of the murder scene. I had a compelling urge to go this time, to do what I should have done last night. I threw on my coat and pulled on my shoes and went down the exit stairs to Ballroom A. On the third floor, in the doorway to the stairs, I looked out into the hotel corridor. I saw Herman Patrick and his plump friend waiting for the elevator. I don't think they saw me, so I sauntered out into the open and tried the doors to Ballroom A. Mr. V, the banquet manager, keeps insisting he locks these doors after each event, but the doorknob turned and I quickly entered the library, closing the door behind me.

The room was dark, but there were lights from Fifth Avenue, car headlights arcing like searchlights. The lights didn't penetrate deeply into the room, but they showed me, as I leaned against the door I'd closed, the figure of a person sitting at a center table. The body was garbed completely in black, including a black veil that partially covered her face. Horrifying.

I must have cried out. I groped for the light switch and jerked it. The little library lamps came on and their lovely yellow glow showed me the most frightening thing I've ever seen. There, in a wing chair, sat the body, its head stiff against the chair back. It was obvious, from the trail of blood, that she'd dragged her fingers across a neatly piled manuscript that rested on the table beside her. Her hair was hidden beneath a hat and the close-twisted black veil, but the skull-like face showed through the thin material.

"DDT?" I whispered, my heart clutching, sickened. I advanced a step or two toward the figure, not knowing what to do.

The clock ticktocked in the room's quietness.

I quaked, but I moved to the figure and stared into the black shroud over her face, praying that she breathed. I put a hand up, but I could feel no warm breath, see no lift in her chest, see no twitch in her curled fingers.

"DDT," I repeated. "Please wake up. Please say something, or move or—"

But the figure just sat there, rigid, smiling behind its shroud.

I touched her forearm, and then I knew. It was waxen under my fingers, cool and slick like snakeskin. I glanced down at the title page of the manuscript: *Hate Letters* by Deirdre Day Tully, Wombat Winner. The wombat is an award given each year by the Writers of Mystery to a "devil's dozen" of best works in different categories. DDT had won hers the first year the awards had been given. And then I noticed the note.

"I have always hated Deirdre Day Tully," it read in blackest ink, "from the time she was born. And at last I have found the courage to kill her. Mourn her not. She will not mourn you. My executors are Ballard, Baldwin & Ballard of New York City." And then, in a smaller, heavier and hastier hand, was scrawled: "I murdered Muriel lake." A black pen had seemingly rolled away from loosened fingers. It lay on the edge of the table, and I almost reached out to move it closer to the manuscript.

And how did I feel then? It's hard to say. I felt a languor in my limbs and a reluctance to hurry. And I felt ashamed somehow, almost responsible for not being able to forestall this pathetic ending. Two nights the clock in this room had struck twelve below my very bed. Two nights in a row, while I showered and sang and ironed, two writers had died. This is a haunted room, I thought, an ill-starred room.

And then I thought that surely, in DDT's letter to me, there had been a call for help that I hadn't understood. She must have been dismally lonely. She must have felt terminally caught between the Muriel Lakes climbing above her and the new writers like me pushing from behind. She had become, in her own mind, a "back number," all future behind her. Augustus Graves, dear diary, is right. There is a time for each of us, and it is always only a short time. Scott Fitzgerald was dead at forty-four, Edgar Allan Poe by forty. I was frightened, then, standing there beside the dead woman. I thought of Kevin and felt a rush of love. I wanted to go to him for comfort; wanted him to hold me. But, of course, I didn't. He and I are mere acquaintances, a conference flirtation. Most of all I felt my own mortality. I saw myself there in that chair. I tasted dirt in my mouth and heard the cosmos crack to take me in. But that was fanciful imagining. What I really heard was the faint whirring of the old clock's mechanism as its pendulum swung back and forth.

Finally I felt a kind of peace for DDT. She wouldn't be sniped at anymore, or pitied, or laughed at. She would be a legend. Her books would be studied in schools and reprinted as classics of their kind. She had made herself immortal.

I stood beside that table, thinking these dark things, and as I did, I glanced around at the cornices of the ballroom. My eyes followed the bookcases placed inside the oblong of the room like a circle drawn inside a rectangle. And then a new thought occurred. Perhaps these rented bookcases sat on casters. The casters are often hidden by wooden skirts and, although heavy, enabled the cases to move at a finger's touch. Even as I thought it my heart leaped and stopped in midair, for a shadow flitted up the wall from behind the bookcase. And a phantom raced along my spine. I may have been a little mad for a moment, terror stricken, but then reason returned. The shadow must have been caused by the headlights of a car passing floors below out on the avenue. But it gave me a real scare. It brought me back to the present and made me decide to leave the library and notify Detective Scott as I should have done immediately. And, no, diary, I didn't try my theory and pull a bookcase. Instead, a coward, I sidled to the double doors, opened one for the hall's light, then turned off the light switch and shut the door behind me.

The corridor was empty. I ran to the front desk and insisted that the woman there ring Scotty's room. With some reluctance she did, and he answered promptly.

He hadn't been asleep—his voice was much too awake—so I didn't apologize for calling him.

"You must come," I said, and told him why. He said he would meet me outside the doors in five minutes. I was to return and stand before them and let no one in until he came.

I did as he ordered, but I hated every minute of being there. Finally Detective Scott arrived, looking tired and in need of a shave.

"I don't want to go in with you," I said. "It isn't nice to see and I'm very tired. Do you need me?"

"Oh, yes," he said. "You discovered her. You have to be with me. I'll have questions." And he opened the door and stood aside for me to go in first.

As I entered, I again saw shadows racing up the walls to my right. I also thought I heard footfalls near the sliding doors into the dining room. But when I flashed on the little table lamps, I realized the shadows were only curves of passing light and that the sliding doors were shut as tight as could be. So I closed my mouth on my foolishness, sat on a small settee and dutifully—and truthfully—answered all of Detective Scott's questions.

It was another hour, almost two o'clock, before I got back here to write this. And it will be three before I sleep.

TWENTY-ONE

10:00 a.m., Thursday

THE NEWS CAUSED a furor. The Hepplewhite was inundated with reporters and minicams, and Herman Patrick called an immediate emergency meeting of the WOM board to discuss the situation. The first vote taken declared the press off-limits, but, of course, they were unable to make the dictum stick.

Eduardo Vinici took the new crisis well. His left hand was strong and steady. Mr. Enders, the Hepplewhite's general manager, wholeheartedly embraced the publicity. He had booked several large groups since the news of the death of Muriel Lake, and he was happily at work creating a "mystery tour" of the rooms in which the victims had stayed and met their deaths. It would be an annual weekend event.

Cecilia and Kevin breakfasted with JoAnn Morris and Gilda Shapiro, and Cecilia found herself, for the first time, the center of the table's attention. She reported how she had found DDT, and the others speculated on what had actually happened as opposed to how it appeared.

"I have a theory," Kevin said, "but none of you will like it because it has no twists."

"Let's hear it," JoAnn Morris said. The writing team wore gray linen walking suits and both sported canes.

"It's exactly what it appears," Kevin said. "There's no mystery. Muriel Lake met Ms Tully in the library that night at DDT's request before Mr. Graves arrived. That's why DDT was out in the hall when Mr. Graves came. She was waiting to see who would discover what she had done. When it turned out to be the publisher who had just rejected her latest book, she thought perhaps she could force him to reconsider. Remember, DDT was desperate. She killed Ms Lake in a jealous fit. Then she was unable to live with herself. And since Graves wouldn't buy *Hate Letters* and he had come clean with Detective Scott, she took sedatives all day yesterday to calm herself down. But all that did was make her despondent and woozy and ridiculous at last night's dinner. And then, after drinking heavily, which made the sleeping pills more effective—or more lethal—she returned to her room, took more pills, wrote her death note and then went back to the scene of the crime to stage her death. What she really meant to do was upstage Muriel's death— take the action away from her rival. And she has, hasn't she?"

"Well, no offense, Kevin, but I hate that scenario," Gilda said. "I wouldn't write it that way."

"All right," Kevin said, shrugging, "then what do you think?"

"I think it's like *And Then There Were None*. Some fiend among us is killing us off one by one."

"Oh, I like that," JoAnn Morris exclaimed. "But he'll have to kill us together, Gilda, because we're one writer."

"That would be a good trick, wouldn't it?" Gilda agreed. "He'd have to be handsome and persuasive. Get us both in bed and kill us with love."

Cecilia was quiet, eating a bowl of fruit salad, listening. Stash Yarrow could get you both in bed, she thought. "The writing at the end of the suicide letter was different," she said finally. "I think DDT killed herself and was discovered by somebody before me, the real killer of Muriel Lake. Then that someone added the confession to the end of the note so that he could get away with what he'd done."

"Oh, golly," Kevin said. "You keep saying 'he.' It makes me squirm."

"Yes, Kevin." JoAnn Morris narrowed her eyes at him. "What were you doing the night Muriel was killed, and last night?"

Kevin pushed out a lip. "Sleeping. Dreaming of Ceci here." And he touched Cecilia's arm affectionately.

"Honestly, none of us are taking this seriously enough," Gilda said. "We've lost two valued members. Two women have died, for heaven's sake. We should show more respect."

"Yes, we should," Cecilia agreed, and she looked around at the others. They were like naughty children who didn't want to grow up. And I'm the same, she thought. I'm having fun, too. She glanced over at the table where Detective Scott, Jonathan Pells, Alice Ludlow, Gordon Gates and Augustus Graves sat, talking among themselves. They looked like grown-ups. Jonathan Pells is a serious writer, she thought. He's not acting like a teenager at a Halloween party.... But then Jonathan reached up and stroked Alice's sleek bob of hair, and Cecilia winced. New widower, no sorrow. New widower, new love. Wasn't that a motivation for murder? Cecilia pushed her chair away. "I'm going back to my room," she announced. "I'm going to skip the morning seminar."

"But that's ours," Gilda protested. "We need your support, Cecilia."

"*I* wouldn't miss it for the world," Kevin said. "Come with me, Ceci."

"Save me a place, then. I'll meet you there." And she left them. She wanted to be alone; she felt smothered, suddenly, by other people. Kevin, for instance. Last night she had wanted to be near him, but this morning he had acted like a boy, not a man. And she kept seeing Deirdre Day Tully in her little room. Had the woman been ingesting sedative pills then? It hadn't seemed so. And she had come running after Cecilia to go up to the attic and witness the capture of the person they'd thought then was the murderer of Muriel Lake. DDT had been full of energy, not doped up with medication. Oh, of course DDT killed herself, Cecilia told herself. The body was so *posed* in the chair, there were no signs of struggle, and the black veil was so properly wound around her face. The whole setting smacked of something DDT would do and, after all, she was in despair at not being able to sell her latest book. But I wonder, Cecilia's mind argued back, if someone tried to murder me with medication, would I know what they were doing before it was too late?

She had reached her room. She unlocked the door, put the Do Not Disturb sign on the outer knob and then closed the door. Then she flopped on her bed, put her arms behind her head and tried to think it out.

But there was someone knocking at her door, ignoring the sign. Someone knocking hard.

"Who is it?" she called.

The knocking was repeated, louder, quicker.

She was afraid, and angry with herself for being afraid.

There was a chain lock she hadn't used, high on the doorframe. She crossed the room, inserted the chain head and opened the door as much as the chain would allow. Herman Patrick stood before her, a roll of paper in his mouth, a stack of folders in his arms.

"Mr. Patrick." She freed the chain.

He came in, put down the folders with a thump and took the roll of paper out of his mouth. "My dear," he said, and sat in her only chair. "Call me Hermione. Everyone does. I never know what people mean when they say 'Mr. Patrick.' We've just had an emergency board meeting. You should have been there."

"But I'm not on the board."

"Still. You're recording secretary. I should have told you, but it's all getting beyond me. It's a travesty, this conference, and I'm the only one trying to keep things together. Trying and failing. Everyone else is having so much fun that it's disgusting." He got out of his chair, went into the bathroom and got himself a glass of water from the tap. "Do you mind, my dear?"

"No," Cecilia said. "How can I help?"

He came back, slicking his hands through his beard and drying them. "Muriel was supposed to make the presentations at the awards dinner tomorrow night. Now it's up to you." He gestured at the pile of folders. "Dossiers on the winners. You're to make up a little card on each of them. No one is to know who the winners are until the announcements are made from the podium. I know the winners, of course, the committees of each award know the winner in their category only, and Muriel, as presenter, knew. That's all, or all who are supposed to. DDT was winning our highest award, the Black Cape. It's such a shame. We should have told her. Then this second tragedy wouldn't have happened. Sometimes the names of winners leak in advance, but they're all supposed to be secret. Oh, hell." He sat there and looked at Cecilia. "You're new. You're the recording secretary. According to Augustus Graves, you're on your way to being prime time. So, Cecilia, my dear, you've been selected to substitute for Muriel." He stopped and took a deep breath. "Will you?"

Cecilia took a deep breath, too. "Then Muriel Lake knew DDT was being honored," she said.

"Of course, Muriel as presenter knew everything. I told you."

"And yet she wouldn't let DDT sit on the dais that first night. DDT told our table she'd asked to and had been rebuffed."

"Muriel didn't like DDT. I don't know why," Herman responded. "She was the only member of the board to vote against DDT getting the Black Cape. But," he said, waggling his fingers dismissively, "Muriel was outvoted for once. Perhaps the only time in her life." He chuckled.

"Mr. Patrick, it should be you in Ms Lake's place, not me. I'm nobody in WOM."

He laughed, a short, sharp laugh. "Ah, my innocent one. We need glamour on awards night, a grand show. I'm a behind-the-scenes player, the real power. For front-of-the-house we want lovely, we want pulchritude, we want elegantly dressed. We don't want Hermione Trick, a bull-dike woman. Forgive my crudeness, Cecilia. I'm frazzled. Just say yes and I'll owe you forever more."

"But what will I wear?" she asked. "I've got nothing spectacular. Mr. Graves complained to me about the way I dress only yesterday."

"Muriel bought a presentation gown," he said. "I've seen it. It's yellow satin, bell skirt, floor-length. It'll be midcalf on you. It'll do splendidly. Try it on for size. If it won't do, or if you're superstitious about wearing her gown, go shopping. Charge it to WOM. We're in no position to protest. But she never wore it, and I think she'd approve of you wearing it." Out of breath he stopped and waited for her reply.

"I don't know what to say, Mr. P—"

"Please, dear. Hermione. Think of me as your sweet, sweet aunt."

"Hermione, what's the name of that friend of yours? I've forgotten."

"Rick Ballard? Dear man. All right now, Cecilia, I've no more time to waste. Just say you will. I've got a thousand things to attend to. The seminar's going on without me, the newspapers want another statement, I have to draft it, Dr. Song has DDT and I'm waiting for the autopsy report. She has a brother in Cincinnati I have to notify—please, dear, ease a fat man's heart and say you'll do this thing. I need you to."

"If you really want me to, I will," she said. "But I'm not used to being in the spotlight."

He pushed himself out of the chair. "Thank God. There are the folders. The scroll contains the confidential list of nominees. The winners are highlighted in yellow. Hide that scroll. No one is to see it but you. Okay?" He was sweating. He ran a palm over his forehead, then wiped it on his trousers.

"Okay," she said.

He leaned over and kissed her cheek. Close, he smelled of sour milk. He left her, mumbling to himself, not looking back.

Cecilia fought back panic. Maybe Muriel had already written the cards, she thought. Maybe they're in that briefcase of hers. I'll go find Detective Scott, ask if he'll let me look, and I'll ask Mr. Pells if I can try on the presentation gown....

Solutions to murder were gone from her mind. Cecilia Burnett was off and running.

CECILIA FOUND Detective Scott in the emptied dining room, sitting with Jonathan Pells and Alice Ludlow. She sat in a nearby chair until he beckoned to her.

"Are you waiting for me?" he asked.

"I want Mr. Pells's permission to see Ms Lake's briefcase," Cecilia said. "I've been asked to substitute for her in announcing the winners tomorrow, and I thought..." She paused before their stares.

"Go on," Jonathan Pells said, and Alice looked inquiringly, as though silently asking: *why you?*

"I thought Ms Lake might have already written out the statements she wanted to make," Cecilia explained, "and if so, I would acknowledge that they were hers and use them exactly as she had planned to."

"How nice of you to think of it," Alice said, and she turned in her chair and crossed one slender leg over the other.

"Yes," Cecilia murmured. "I know nothing of the winners, and Ms Lake did all the work."

"I'll take you up," Pells agreed, "as soon as Scotty here is through with me."

Cecilia took a deep breath. "I have another request to ask of you," she said, but she looked at Alice Ludlow instead of the writer.

"Well?" Pells waited.

"Mr. Patrick said Ms Lake bought a gown to wear. I hadn't, of course, expected to be standing in for her—"

"You want to wear Muriel's gown?" Alice interrupted. "That's a little bloody, isn't it?"

Cecilia nodded. "Herman, you know, Hermione, said I should ask. But WOM will buy me one if—"

"I think it might be nice," Scotty said. "Ms Burnett, here, would only be a substitute for Muriel. It would be a tribute. What do you say, Jonathan?"

Jonathan looked at Alice. "Generosity isn't WOM's strong point. I'd hate to see the bargain-basement dress they'd buy."

"Oh, I'd buy it," Cecilia said. "Then they'd—"

"It's okay with me," Jonathan said. "If the dress fits, wear it."

"Under the circumstances, it's by far the best thing," Alice Ludlow agreed. "Why don't I go to Jonathan's suite with you?"

"Thank you," Cecilia said. "I'd like your help."

"Am I excused?" Alice asked Scotty

"The memorial service is scheduled for four," he said. "In the library. Press invited, of course. See you then." He turned back to Jonathan. "Okay, let's go through it one more time."

Alice took Cecilia's elbow and steered her away. "It's sad," she said. "Scotty and Jonathan used to be friends."

"Detective Scott doesn't really think Jonathan murdered his wife, does he?"

"I don't know," Alice answered. "But now he's got to tie in DDT's death if he can. He'll be taking handwriting samples before the memorial service and after, I warn you."

"Oh," Cecilia thought aloud, "then whoever doesn't show up will be suspect."

"No one's supposed to know. I do because Scotty already took ours."

"Poor Detective Scott," Cecilia said. "He's not having much fun, is he? And poor Mr. Pells."

They were quiet in the elevator, surrounded by strangers. Alice spoke again once they'd entered the hall to the Franklin Delano Roosevelt Suite. "Don't be sorry for Jonny," she said. "He and Muriel hadn't been in love for a long time."

"Still," Cecilia said, "I barely knew her and I feel bereft."

"I don't."

They were at the door marked by a white-framed plaque. Alice produced a card key. Cecilia noticed but said nothing. Alice inserted it, turned the knob, and the door swung back.

Cecilia stepped in. "When I'm famous, will hotels give me such handsome rooms?"

Alice cocked an eyebrow. "You have to ask. You'll learn that. You have to know what can be offered and then demand it. That's one of the ways the haves keep the have-nots out. Have-nots don't know what to ask for."

Cecilia wandered around the sitting room. "I'd never think to ask for the Roosevelt Suite."

"Now you will," Alice said. She led the way to the bedroom.

"I'm not sure I'm going to feel right wearing her dress."

"It's just fabric. Muriel only bought it. She never wore it."

"You didn't like her, did you?" Cecilia waited in the middle of the room for Alice to go into the closet.

Alice did and flipped through the assembled outfits. "I liked her," she called out into the room. "I was her editor before she went with Tombstone." She backed out of the closet with folds of yellow satin covered in plastic sheeting. "And there's long gloves and shoes to go with it—if the shoes fit."

"I have a pair of heels," Cecilia said. "White pumps. They'll do. Are you in love with Jonathan Pells?"

Alice sat in a boudoir chair and smiled at the directness of the question. "I used to be. I want to be."

Cecilia was embarrassed she'd asked. "Will you wait, please, while I try it on?"

"Go to it. There's a bag of jewelry here, too, clipped under the hanger. Ah, an emerald pendant on a choker of seed pearls and earrings to match. Very nice."

"Oh, I couldn't wear her jewelry," Cecilia insisted, struggling to get the dress free of the plastic.

"I would," Alice said, and she held an earring to her hair and looked in the dresser mirror. "Oh, yes, I would. And have no guilt. Things are only things, Cecilia. Nothing belongs to a person once the person isn't there to be belonged to."

"Well, of course you're right," Cecilia agreed as she pulled off her loose-weave sweater and then stepped out of her skirt.

And then they were both quiet again as Cecilia raised the gown over her head and pulled it gently. With her arms imprisoned upward and her eyes blind against the inside of the gown, Cecilia had the thought that now she was defenseless and that Alice Ludlow, if she chose, could murder her any number of ways. I'd be the third mystery writer to die, she thought, and things always happen in threes, so they say....

The gown was on and was almost a perfect fit. It was an elegant dress, more sophisticated than she was used to, and she thought she didn't become it. But she resolved, unconsciously chewing her lower lip, to wear it if Herman/Hermione thought it would do. To save WOM money, she thought that he would pronounce it perfect.

She turned to Alice. "What do you think?"

Alice leaned back in her chair and crossed her legs. "Well, little one, it's too old for you. You don't have the maturity to wear it. But it fits, and if you pinned up your hair and wore the jewelry and a little make-up, that would help."

Cecilia smiled. "Thanks, Alice, you're honest. I appreciate that." Cecilia moved around, turning this way and that, swishing the skirt. Her hands found slash pockets on either side. In the right-hand one her fingers felt a piece of paper. As she studied herself, she balled the piece of paper and poked it into the pocket's corner.

"I'll take it off now," she said, and reached behind her neck to loosen the zipper.

Alice nodded. "And then you can go through the briefcase and see if there's anything you can use. It's on the other side of the dresser along the wall."

The telephone rang and Alice answered it. Cecilia was shaking her arms free of the sleeves. Alice lifted a hand for Cecilia to stop. "Yes, Hermione, she looks a dream. Come on over and see for yourself." Alice replaced the receiver in its cradle and shrugged. "Hermione is on his way. Better wait and let him make the final decision."

Cecilia pulled the sleeves back into position, re-zipped the gown and located the briefcase. She laid it on the dresser top and began riffling through the different folders. Almost immediately she found a thin band of index cards with a label: Nominees/Winners.

"Oh, maybe I'm in luck," she said, and looked in the mirror for Alice.

But Alice was up and walking through the sitting room to answer a knock on the door. "It's open," she heard Alice call as she went.

Alone, Cecilia pulled out the scrap of paper from the gown's pocket. She thought it would be a tailor's mark or an inspection notice. But still...

It was none of those things. It was a bit of torn, lined notepaper, accordion-pleated, and written in scrawled faded pencil was a number: 5951482. With no time to consider, Cecilia pushed the paper into her purse. Perhaps it was nothing, she thought. But it could be a telephone number of Muriel's secret lover, or the code to a bank vault with all the answers....

"Just what the hell's going on!" It was Gilda Shapiro, stamping her walking cane. JoAnn Morris was close behind her. "This will not do, Cecilia. It will not do at all."

Cecilia set the banded pile of index cards aside. "Hello," she said.

Herman Patrick was with the two writers, his face flushed but stern. "Don't listen to their cat talk, Cecilia. It will be you and no one else. You're guileless, guiltless. You're the one the organization will hate the least after it's all over. I have decided."

"Well, screw you," Gilda said. "*We* should do it. After all we've been to WOM, this is a high insult. We will do it, or we will resign and take half the members with us, all the women. Really, Cecilia, we're surprised at you."

"Offended," JoAnn added. "You're nobody. You've just joined. Who do you think you are?"

Cecilia was afraid to sit and crush the gown, so she backed away as far as she could get and unzipped the back and began again struggling out of the tight sleeves. She said nothing.

Herman protectively stood in front of her, his back to her. "Listen, you cats," he said. "*I* asked Cecilia to do this. It was decided by the board."

"We're on the board!" JoAnn and Gilda screamed together.

"Well, you weren't there!" Herman Patrick screamed back.

"We were busy," Gilda said in a more reasonable tone, and JoAnn Morris snapped her head in emphatic agreement.

"Too busy is out of luck," said Herman. "The board decided unanimously that this was the best way out of a difficult situation. DDT obviously can't do it, Muriel can't do it, anyone else would be hated, get the newcomer. That's the way it went down. If you don't like it—"

JoAnn Morris folded her arms across her chest. "How many votes were there? Yours and who else?"

"Jonathan, Rick Ballard and me."

"Jonathan!"

"He's not on the board, you creep."

"He voted for his wife," Herman said. "And I hold proxy rights to DDT's vote and Stash's. So stuff it, sisters. You weren't there. And, anyway, it's best. If you girls did it, you'd never win a best book, much less a nomination ever again. You'd be hated forever. Get smart."

"Get dead," Gilda said. "And you, too, Cecilia."

They stamped their canes together, turned on their heels and marched out. The front door, in the next room, slammed behind them.

"Whoo," Herman Patrick said. "Just one big happy family, that's us."

"I'll say," Alice agreed. "Jealousy and murder, hate letters and adultery. Just your ordinary writers' group, Peyton Place revisited."

"I think I'm going to cry," Cecilia said. She was out of the dress and back in her summer sweater and skirt.

"Don't get sad and don't get mad," Herman Patrick urged. "And don't get even. Get ahead. That's the best revenge."

"Oh, I like that," Alice said. "Chin up, Cecilia, and welcome to the real world."

Cecilia picked up her purse and slung it over her shoulder. "Right," she said. "I'm going to do it, Hermione, even if it kills me."

Alice and Herman Patrick looked at each other as she left.

"Maybe it will," Alice said, gathering up her bag.

"Better her than us, my dear," Herman said, traipsing out with her. "That's another *bon mot* worth remembering."

TWENTY-TWO

11:30 a.m., Thursday

CECILIA WAS AWARE that the seminar featuring JoAnn M. S. Gold was proceeding without her. But she preferred to be alone in her room now, so she could think.

She stretched out on her bed, head propped against the headboard, and began writing in her diary.

How quickly you can begin to know a person if you really look. Stash Yarrow, for instance. I think he is just a writer trying to fulfill the male image, not really a sexual satyr. Stash is a hardworking writer and maybe he doesn't have the time to keep a love affair or a marriage afloat. He's married to his work. He had no reason to kill Muriel Lake. I think publicity motivates Stash—publicity and sales. I shall try to be more like him.

And Jonathan Pells. If he wanted to murder his wife, he would sensibly do it in private on their estate, or on a research trip to somewhere remote. Then he could control most of the variables. He wouldn't have had to worry that the gossip concerning his failed career would prejudice people into thinking he was guilty of murder. In all honesty, I don't think Jonathan is terribly sorry Muriel is dead, and he won't brood over her death too long. His luck has already changed; I suppose he's rich now that her assets and copyrights are his. He's letting himself be controlled and guided by Alice Ludlow because although he may be a strong writer, he's a weak man. I predict Jonathan and Alice will marry when his new book is ready for publication. In the attendant publicity, his book will succeed wildly and he'll spend the rest of his life working with and relying on Alice. In the short term he'll enjoy the notoriety he'll receive as the widower of Muriel Lake.

At this point, Cecilia stopped and copied the number she had found in Muriel's dress. Then she picked up her telephone receiver, dialed 9 and then the number, just to see what would happen. It was a working New York City number. It rang and rang, unanswered. Beneath the number she wrote: "Try again. Bank vault? Ask J. Pells." Then she turned to a fresh page and continued to record her thoughts.

Herman/Hermione isn't a killer, although there is more to him than meets the eye. He doesn't really like women, he prefers the company of men, and he can stand up to the double barrage of JoAnn M. S. Gold when he has to. And he bearded Gordon Gates the other day and got a chance to move into hardcover with Haunting House, so he's got moxie. But ML's death in no way benefits him. Nor does DDT's.

Rick Ballard simply seems retiring and sweet. I'm not even sure he's a writer.

That leaves my two friends, JoAnn and Gilda. They might profit from the deaths of Muriel Lake and DDT in terms of less competition, but that's tenuous, isn't it? JoAnn and Gilda are doing all right. There's no reason to murder a rival on the chance of doing better.

Cecilia chewed the end of her pen. The trouble with the murder of Muriel Lake was that no one, really, had a driving motive and almost anyone could have taken the opportunity. The means, the disguised dictionary-safe, worried her, too.

Who would know about the safe except an intimate—Jonathan or maybe Scotty? Muriel didn't give away her secrets; she kept them. She liked secrets.

Oh, that's it, Cecilia thought. That's got to be it. The secret was shared by Muriel and her killer only. The murderer was an intimate of that secret, and here's the thing—the secret wasn't Muriel's at all, but his! We've all been looking in the wrong place—at Muriel's life and private things. And the secret isn't there. It's in the murderer's "secret box." Oh, I'm right. I know I'm right....

She swung off the bed, excited. She pulled open the drawer of the table beside the bed, hauled out the heavy New York City telephone directory and looked up the telephone number of Tyrone Scott. It was there; although it wasn't the number she'd found in Muriel's pocket. Then she found a number for Alice Ludlow, Gordon Gates and Augustus Graves. None of the numbers matched the one Muriel had hidden. She'd go to Scotty now, she decided, turn over the number, explain how she'd found it. Maybe it was a vault combination written in some kind of code.

Maybe the number was irrelevant. But she had to solve its mystery. She'd go to Herman Patrick and ask for a list of all the participants at the conference, including their telephone numbers. She would bet her next book contract that the number in Muriel's dress pocket would be on that printout.

She rang DDT's room and Scotty answered. "I thought you'd be there," she said. "Can I come to see you? I have another clue, I think."

"Sure. You're becoming a fund of information, Ms Burnett. If you're not careful, I'm going to start suspecting you."

"I thought you already did," she said, and rang off.

TWENTY-THREE

12:30 p.m., Thursday

A RUMOR OF THE IMPENDING merger of Haunting House Press and Tombstone Books spread quickly during lunch. The new company would be called GravesGate, and according to Alice Ludlow, only financial details remained to be worked out for the merger to become official.

"They found out that they liked each other," she told a group consisting of JoAnn and Gilda, Herman and his shadow Rick, Cecilia and Stash.

"Incredible," Stash said. "I thought crocodiles fished alone."

"Matter of sink or swim for Gordon," Alice responded. "He'll benefit enormously. And Augie will become a major publisher in one stroke. He takes on debt, yes, but he gets real depth. He'll have all of Muriel's backlist, and all of DDT's."

"Not good from a writer's point of view," Herman said. "It makes one less market to sell to."

"And it becomes a take-our-offer or don't sell," JoAnn contributed. "I don't like it at all."

"Listen, darlings," Alice began, "there'll be bigger paychecks for all of you, and better-managed publicity campaigns with bigger pushes. I'm terribly enthusiastic. It's the beginning of the big time for the mystery. No more getting lost in the genre shuffle. The mystery, with this merger, goes mainstream.''

"I doubt it," Herman said. "But along with you, I will hope.''

"DDT died at the wrong time then. Is that what you're saying, Alice?'' Stash asked.

"Everyone dies at the wrong time," Cecilia said unexpectedly, and the table laughed.

After the argument in Muriel's suite, Cecilia had thought she would be ignored by the writing team of JoAnn M. S. Gold, but JoAnn and Gilda had waved her over when she'd entered Ballroom B for lunch. It was as though the heated words had never been said. Herman was sitting with them; everyone at the table seemed determined to be amiable.

Kevin had come over, hurt that Cecilia hadn't made it to the seminar. "All through it I was conscious of your empty chair, Ceci. I had no fun and I couldn't concentrate, and JoAnn and Gilda had interesting things to say.''

She'd told him she had been asked to substitute for Muriel Lake at the awards ceremony the following night and would be wearing Muriel's presentation gown.

"Oh, rats. Now you're too important for me, I guess," he said. "And I liked you, too.''

"Oh, stop," she said. "There's a movie tonight after dinner, no speaker. *Casablanca*. Let's see it together.''

"That's more like it," he said. "And I'll bring you my manuscript so that you can read yourself to sleep."

"Okay, Kevin. But if it stinks—"

"Come on, Ceci. I'll take it on the chin like a man."

And then he'd gone off to another table to sit with people she didn't know, and she soon realized that she missed him.

After lunch Dr. Song addressed them on the death of Deirdre Day Tully. She had died, he said, of natural causes. She had been taking a heart stabilizer and booster for years. And she must have left her dosage at home, because there was virtually none in her system. She had been drinking rather more than she was used to. He had consulted with her doctor; Ms Tully was allowed three ounces of sherry a day. She had consumed, the night of her death, three times that amount of hard liquor and wine. Her heart, overexcited, had staggered under its burden, bumped to a halt and been unable to recover. Without medicine, without help, death had come. She might have meant to do it; as to that he couldn't, and wouldn't, speculate. There were no signs of foul play and no reason to suspect any. She had no family. He had spoken to her executors. Her estate had been willed as an indigent writers' home. It was an old Victorian mansion in New Hampshire on several acres of rocky land and was in need of modernization. Her monies and copyrights would go into a trust fund for the haven's upkeep.

The members of WOM accepted the news. The death of the elderly writer had saddened rather than excited them. Those who knew DDT, or most of them, thought she had deliberately staged her end and had meant to do it. Few considered the possibility that Deirdre Day Tully had murdered Muriel Lake to be realistic. She had the spirit to do it, they said, but not the strength. She had penned the confessing post-script in delirium; in her death throes. Such was the general consensus.

So after lunch the writers went their separate ways and planned to gather together in the "library" at four for the memorial service for their two colleagues.

THE SERVICE WASN'T RELIGIOUS. The little library lamps were turned to half brilliance, the gas fireplace was lit and two tall white candles in silver candle-sticks were placed on a reading table at the front of the room to represent the departed. Around the candles were all the bouquets that had been purchased by the members of WOM from the florist salesman of two days ago. They had been delivered that morning and banked around the table.

Everyone attending was asked to write the post-script to DDT's last letter before proceeding in, and Detective Scott collected them. Herman Patrick stood behind the table to deliver a double eulogy. He called both women "the great ladies of American mystery." TV cameras recorded it, print reporters took their notes. There was none of the party atmosphere that had existed the day before.

After Herman Patrick finished, others who wanted to speak lined up. Each took a turn telling a memory or two, a little anecdote about DDT, a simple incident about Muriel Lake.

Cecilia thought it interesting that because of DDT's age and former eminence, she was always mentioned first. Muriel Lake, younger, more commercial, but with quantitatively a smaller body of work, came second. Cecilia knew that DDT would be pleased. Cecilia didn't speak because she had hardly known the women. She kept busy writing down the thoughts and memories of those who did speak.

And then it was over. Technicians rolled up their cords and many of the writers went on to have a drink before dinner. Jonathan, Augustus and Gordon were interviewed, but that was all.

Again Cecilia sought the comfort of her room. She showered and changed one skirt and summer sweater for another and then lay down on her bed and fell into a deep sleep. Only Kevin's knocking saved her from missing dinner.

"I'm coming, I'm coming," she called, and opened the door to him.

"Here it is," he said, handing over a brown paper bag. "*Sudden Departure*. It's not wrapped in a blue box like Muriel's, but it's all there."

"Oh, I hate doing this, Kevin," she said. "I so want you to do well and I'm afraid... Well, writing's not as easy as it looks, you know. Oh, Kevin. I'll read it tonight after the movie, okay?"

"Yeah. I just don't want to hold it all through the evening. I'd rather hold you."

Cecilia smiled, a little. "See you later then."

"Good."

"Well," she said, and smiled weakly after he had closed the door. She looked at the manuscript, its corners creased in the limp brown bag. It's going to be horrible, she thought, and I'm going to have to tell him.

TWENTY-FOUR

8:30 p.m., Thursday

THE DINNER WAS ALMOST DULL. Cecilia and Kevin sat at a table with Herman Patrick and Rick Ballard. Herman used the occasion to tell Cecilia about the various nominees for the Wombat Awards.

Stanislas Yarrow had somehow learned he was receiving WOM's best novel award, a black bat for *The Denver Dossier*. "But please don't congratulate him before the event," Herman cautioned. "He's not supposed to know, but he does. Muriel must have tipped him. He told me that if 'best bat' isn't in his hands tomorrow night, there'll be a third murder at this conference, namely me."

"Oh, I understand," Cecilia said. She ate her carrots and peas, which were mixed with mint jelly because lamb was being served. She left the meat untouched and filled up on the vegetables, salad and bread. She also managed to eat all of the dessert, which was chocolate sponge cake cut into slices that resembled a pistol in profile. The sweet sauce that completed the effect was red raspberry that pooled, appropriately, over and under the muzzle of the "gun." There was no after-dinner speaker, so the cof-

fee arrived with dessert, and for the first time that
week it was hot.

Although the room was relatively quiet, Cecilia
sensed an atmosphere of tension. It was like a haze,
collecting slowly. But where was it coming from? she
wondered. Who was the thunder god?

Cecilia was actually glad that things were quieter.
She found herself distracted from the murder of Muriel Lake by worries of her new duties tomorrow evening. Her mind wouldn't settle on Kevin, who
thankfully was quiet beside her, or on the tidbits of
information that Herman and his friend ticked off for
her. Nor had she found the time to savor her new status with Tombstone Books. She realized that she was
tired, worn out by the fevered pace at which the conference had run. She had her tape recorder going,
something she rarely used because she didn't trust it.
It was voice-activated, and she never knew for sure if
it was on or not. She promised herself she would spend
a part of tomorrow listening again to what Herman
and his friend were saying now. Despite their advice,
she still expected to read from the cards Muriel had
compiled. To do anything else, Cecilia thought, would
be disrespectful.

At dinner's end she was glad to leave and stroll with
Kevin into Ballroom A for the showing of *Casablanca*. They were among the first to arrive, and when
they took a settee near the end of the room, Cecilia
noticed the hotel bellman, yesterday's "red herring,"
moving around the room. He straightened a chair

here, set an ashtray there, put down bowls of pop-
corn on the library tables. I've seen him everywhere,
she thought, too tired to do more than remark it to
herself. His father killed a man here, and now the son
is getting a second chance. She watched Romeo Popoi going about his work. She wondered how his father's crime had changed him. The killer instinct is in
all of us, she mused. We humans admit that. So we
bury it with taboos and punishment. But some of us
don't shrink from its possibility; some of us understand that it's not some fantastic never-never thing but
an alternative, waiting if we ever need it. Some of us
aren't surprised when murder happens.

Ballroom A began to fill, and Cecilia turned her attention to the curved bookcases forming a circle
around the room. She sought again the shadows that
had frightened her last night, when automobiles had
rolled down Fifth Avenue with their headlights on. But
tonight she couldn't catch a single shadow flitting up
the walls. She thought it might be because the reading
lamps were on. When the lights are off, she thought,
I'll see the phantom shadows. If I don't, it means there
was someone behind those bookcases the night DDT
died. It was something she sincerely didn't want to be
so—

"Kevin," she said.

He shifted beside her. "I was almost dozing," he
said.

"Solving murders is hard work," she said, teasing.

He hid a yawn behind his hands. "Not solving them is even harder. You know, I've racked my brain, racked it out, really. And guess what I've concluded?"

"I have no idea."

"I hate to say it, but here goes. DDT did do it, after all. Not a satisfactory ending, but she must have. She admitted it on her death bed."

"Oh, no, you'll have to do better than that," she argued. "Did you get your handwriting sample taken?"

"Yeah, and I didn't like it. I found it offensive. That detective asked me to write 'I killed Muriel Lake.' It gave me the chills. Did you?"

"Everybody did. And, yes, it was horrible. I think that's why the conversation's so dull tonight."

"Maybe. I've been sitting here, wishing this whole week was behind us and we were into next week and I was taking you to a movie for real."

"Oh, let's do, Kevin. Let's be friends. I'd like that."

"I want us to be more than friends, Ceci. I haven't been kidding, you know, this week."

But then the film began and the lights dimmed. People excused themselves, shuffling past Cecilia and Kevin in the dark. He took her hand and held it, the room quieted down and once, when Rick toasted Ilsa with a "Here's looking at you, kid," Kevin raised her hand to his lips and kissed it lightly. Her hand squeezed his in friendly return, but she was worried. His manuscript was waiting for her in her room, and if it was as bad as she thought it was going to be, she could never see him again.

In the dark she sought the walls for shifting shadows. They were everywhere, gray and grayer, fading, swelling. Movie-made, most of them, certainly. But all of them? Were some of those mysterious slippings and slidings created by the cars surging three stories below? She didn't think so. Someone had been hidden in this room last night. And that someone is here tonight, close by, near. I almost caught him in the act—he hid. Well, I didn't see you, she shouted in her mind. So leave me alone!

Romeo Popoi passed on his way out. Cecilia shivered in her seat and averted her gaze from his.

ILSA HAD FLOWN AWAY, rain streaked the window of the little plane, and Rick and the police commissioner walked across the tarmac and disappeared into fog. Cecilia would have preferred remaining wrapped in the glow of it, but Kevin was impatient.

"I know you're tired, but you promised," he said as the reading lamps came up and the screen went white. "And I want to give *Sudden Departure* to Mr. Graves while he still remembers me. So please don't say you're too tired. You can skim. I'll give you a little Scotch, I'll sit very quiet, it'll only take an hour or so. Just read the beginning, a piece of the middle and—"

"Let's go do it, then," she said, and waved quick good-nights to the others. She noticed Detective Scott watching her leave with appraising eyes. But it can't be him! she thought. Her mind turned to other things as she left with Kevin.

She was shy in her room at first. It felt so intimate, the double bed in a midtown hotel, alone with a man who professed to desire her. She wasn't used to it.

Kevin recognized her discomfort and made a face at her. "All right," he said. "Here's what I'm going to do, blow by blow. I'm going into your bathroom to fill two tumblers with water. I'll add a little Scotch to yours and a little more to mine. Then I'm going to sit in that chair over there and read your copy of Muriel's *Desperate* and not say a word, not even look at you. I want you to get comfortable on your bed and read."

Cecilia smiled at him, grateful. "I'll make notes regarding questions, praise or complaints."

"And, listen, thanks, Ceci, sincerely."

She took the tumbler and tasted the bitter bite of the Scotch. She rarely drank alcohol, but tonight she wanted it. The manuscript sat on the table beside her bed; the stack of white pages was comforting. Also on the table was a small bulb-shaped vase with five fading daisies, the table lamp and the brown hotel telephone.

Kevin sat across the room. He set his Scotch on the dresser, picked up the copy of *Desperate*, and then glanced at her before opening the book.

She had been watching him, sipping her weak drink. "Here I go," she said, curling her legs under her and propping her body against the headboard. She pushed the pillow behind the small of her back and adjusted it to give some support to her elbow.

Kevin glanced at his wristwatch. "Ten-thirty-five. Start reading."

She bent her head to the first page. And instantly she was engrossed. *Sudden Departure* had a clever beginning, it was intriguingly plotted, and its characters were fresh and well drawn. Cecilia was astonished and embarrassed at her earlier doubts. Unconsciously she sighed a little. Kevin must be a great writer, she thought. This is first-class work. But can he keep it up? She sipped at her drink and read on, lost in the pages, time and tiredness forgotten.

And then it seemed only moments had passed, although it was clearly much later—she heard the clock strike twelve. A long, resounding chime, deep-chested, melodious, it boomed beneath her bed. It brought her out of the manuscript and back to reality, and she trembled. She knew that sound well now, *the death knell*, and yet it always surprised her. It brought the first night back and the second, and the guilt and the horror.

Each time it rings someone dies.

Cecilia tensed, waiting for the second strum. She kept her head down and her eyes on the page because she didn't want to have to explain things to Kevin. The *bonnnggg* came, floated under the bed like a wraith and died slowly.

Turning over a page took such effort. She was aware of her breathing—deep and slow. She pretended to read on, but she was caught by the chimes. She would have to wait, counting in her head to twelve before she would be released.

The third came. She closed her eyes. Soon it will be over, she thought, and no one will die tonight.

The fourth toll crashed beneath her. The even-numbered sounds were louder than the odd, as though the pendulum, angry that its first swing hadn't satisfied the mechanism that drove it, leaped harder into the opposing arc of its sway. Then, relaxing—*bonnnggg*—it fell back the other way, weaker, frustrated, and then *bonnnggg* again with all its might.

Seven...

Eight...

With the ninth reverberation a dread thought stiffened her. Visibly she shook and couldn't stop. She tried to dispel it, to disavow it, to *repudiate* the thought.

What if Kevin hadn't written this book?

Bonnnggg!

What if this is the lost novel of Muriel Lake?

No. *Yes*. No.

Bonnnggg-yes.

Her arms lifted and crossed her chest. The movement was slow and hard to make. Her hands, ice-cold, clutched at the cotton of her summer sweater.

Bonnnggg.

The last tolling. The pendulum gave up the ghost and retreated to the center of the clock's etched-glass facing. It would rest now for twelve hours.

Cecilia's hand, unable to grip any longer, fell away from her shoulder. Like a dull student, slowly her mind found conviction, told her what she already knew: this manuscript on her lap was Muriel Lake's. Cecilia knew. She was an ardent fan. She had read everything except *Desperate* because she bought her books in paperback and so waited out the year of their hardcover release.

Each page screamed at her in Muriel's voice, Muriel's style, Muriel's trademark techniques. The way she laid down a line, building always to the tension of a sentence, a paragraph, a scene. The way she avoided the usual phrases and carved out her own, new ones. The way she created fresh images by connecting new associations, new words, by hyphen—all Muriel Lake.

Never Kevin Wilder.

The manuscript turned in to Augustus Graves in a Tiffany-blue box hadn't been Muriel Lake's *Unforgivable Sin*. The terrible, disappointing thing that Augustus Graves had taken away that night must have been Kevin's novel, the title pages simply switched. And here, in Cecilia's cold, slow hands was the book that had cost Gordon Graves a million dollars and Muriel Lake her life....

She looked up at Kevin, whom she had started to love. Her hands fell away at her sides, a page fluttered off her lap on its own. She couldn't move her limbs. Her mind worked, though, and her eyes.

Across the room in the chair he was looking at her, somber. There was a new maturity in his face, a strength she hadn't seen before.

"I see," he said. She could hear him, but she couldn't turn away or move or answer.

"I see," he said, "what I wanted to see. It isn't going to work the way I wanted it to, after all. You can tell. And if you can, *they* can."

He sipped from his glass, closed Muriel's *Desperate* and set it back on the dresser. Then he stretched, stood and began to pace. His face was boyish again. There was a sparkle in his eyes and a warm grin on his mouth. "I'm not going to get away with it, am I?"

"No," she sighed. It was hard to form the word. Her lips were stiff; her whole body was very cold. She barely breathed. And yet her mind flew, still clear, still quick. He's drugged me. Probably DDT's medication. Or a heart muscle relaxant. Something he found in her pillboxes.…

"I met Muriel at a WOM party in January," he said, pacing, smiling. "She liked men, as you know. And she liked me, liked my looks. I could tell. So I flattered her and I flirted and I asked her to come out and have a little supper. Cheap, you know, I said. I'm a struggling writer. But come, please."

He glanced at Cecilia, staring dumbly from the bed, and then shrugged, almost apologetic for his charm. "She came," he went on, marching up and down along the carpet beyond the bed. "And we had fun. I said I wanted to see more of her, wanted to show her more of me. So we went to my apartment, made love. The very first night. She was hot and I laid it on. That's one of the tricks, Ceci. The first time you make love to a woman, give it a hundred and ten percent. Women always judge you by the first time. That's the one they remember. So I worked at it, you know, and I pleased her.

"I pleased her so much that we agreed to meet here at the Hepplewhite in a room she rented once a week when she came into town. Wednesday matinees, we called our little assignations. Of course I asked her to help me, to take a look at my work, the way I asked you. Like you, she was nice about it, she said yes. And she was honest, too, the way you would have been if you had read my novel. The way Augustus Graves was. She said it wouldn't do. It wasn't any good and I'd have to try again. So I asked to read hers, so I could set them side by side, I said, and see what she did right and I did wrong. But she wouldn't do that. I could read her earlier books, she said. Nobody could see *Unforgivable Sin* in manuscript except her publisher and editor.

"And that's when the idea of the switch came to me, full-blown, just like that, in the Franklin Delano Roosevelt Suite right upstairs. That's the room she always booked. She told me about her 'signature' things, how that helped establish a 'recognition factor.' She told me to find my own signatures and to stay with them. She always turned over her manuscripts in a Tiffany-blue box, for instance, the title page taped to the outside, and then another one inside. She didn't put her name at the top of each page the way most writers do, or the title of the work. That was another of the ways her manuscripts were different from other novelists.

"So it was easy to switch the title pages after she was dead and put my *Sudden Departure* where her *Unforgivable Sin* had been. I knew Gordon Gates would have to publish it. He'd paid big bucks for it already. And with Muriel dead he'd recover his investment easily. What a legacy, I thought, for me. My novel to be published as the last words of the great Muriel Lake. And I had, to be released under my name, the real thing, a million-dollar novel as my coming-out party.... Are you relaxed now, Ceci? You look very relaxed. Can you answer me?"

She looked at him but didn't try to answer. I must save my strength, she thought. I must find a way to get out.

"Can you blink, Ceci? Answer me one blink for yes, two blinks for no."

It was easy not to obey. Her eyelids were frozen in place, folded up into their sockets so that she could stare at him and see all the things he was.

"All right, you're mad at me," he said conversationally. "I'm sorry because I liked you a lot, but it can't be helped. I'm going to get away with it, Ceci. At least the murders. I'm going to get away with murder! But I won't get the novel. You've made me see that. People will know. It's a no go." He waggled a finger, thinking it out. "That was the one variable, Muriel's recognition factor. She'd really worked on it. She'd gotten it down. That's how you came into it. Ms Average Reader. Okay, better-than-average reader. I hadn't counted on your work being so good. You don't look like a great mystery writer, Ceci. You should have worked much harder on that the way she did. Looks count."

He sat on the edge of the bed. Her feet were still tucked under her legs. She couldn't feel them.

"I talked with Detective Scott tonight," Kevin said. "He thinks it's Augustus Graves, but he's not going to do anything until he can put a case together, and that won't be until after this conference is history. I tried to make it DDT. I don't know why that one didn't work. DDT was a natural killer. But nobody bought it. So now it's you, kid. Everything in threes, just like you said."

She tried to say, "You put something in my drink," but only a mew issued from her throat. She was warm now, comfortably warm, although she'd been ice-cold just minutes ago. She was very relaxed, like a rag doll, all seams tight along the edges, all flannel within.

He moved up the bed, stretched her limp arms wide, took her in his arms. "I'm going to kill you, Ceci," he said tenderly.

He laid her back, her head against the bedstead, her arms at her sides. She tried to resist, to twist beneath the hands that now caressed her breasts, that teased her. But her muscles wouldn't respond to the demands of her mind. She twitched and lay open to his hands.

He took Muriel's manuscript from her lap, stacked the pages together and poked it back into the crumpled brown bag on the floor. From his trouser pocket he pulled out thin rubber gloves. He slipped them on, went into the bathroom and found a towel. He took away her glass and his, washed them and set them back on the glass shelf in the bathroom over the sink. He whistled gently as he worked.

Then he returned to her side. "How lovely you are, and how nice, Ceci. I liked you so much."

And then his fingers moved to the first button of her sweater, and the second and the third. As he loosened the brown plastic circles from their nooses, he smoothed the material away. Then the snap of her bra, between her breasts was exposed. He smiled, and with a movement of his hand, released it.

Her breasts were bare to him. The sweater lay wide open, its sides along her submissive arms. "They'll know," she wanted to tell him, but her lips wouldn't move. She groaned, trying to.

He unbuttoned the waist of her skirt and freed the side zipper. "You're a great note-taker, Ceci. That's the one thing everyone knows about you. I've thought it out and that's what you'll do. A long letter to Herman Patrick confessing everything. You killed Muriel Lake, you see. You went down to meet her. You'd asked her for a blurb for your new book and she said she wanted to talk to you about it. So you went down and she insulted you, told you the book was no good. She wouldn't endorse it and she claimed she was going to talk to her lover, your publisher, Augustus Graves, and ask him to withdraw it.

"You discovered the book-safe. She had it with her because she wanted to discuss something about her contract with Mr. Graves, who was expected shortly. But you became violently angry. In an instant, without thinking, you slammed her with it. You hadn't meant to kill her, you'll say, you were just mad, just flinging out. But she fell and began to bleed and then you were afraid she would get you for assault, so you decided you had to finish the job and make it look like an accident. So you banged her again, well aimed and very hard, and then you adjusted her body and threw some books at it. And then you discovered that the bookcases swung out easily on casters. You stood up on a chair and hauled the bookcase down on her.

"Deirdre Day Tully then chose to make her appearance and you were forced to hide behind the bookcase. You were scared then, little darling girl, but you hid, there between the wall and the back of the bookcases, and DDT left. And then you ran along the walls toward the sliding doors into Ballroom B and almost got out of there. But that's when Graves came in, so you had to wait again, hunkered down like an animal. But then he left, too, and finally you were able to slip into Ballroom B and into the corridor and back to your room, where you slept as if you were dead. Yes, dead, Cecilia.''

His hand caressed her knee, and then she felt it moving up toward her thigh. She could see and hear and feel, but she couldn't respond. She turned her eyes to the left, toward the side table, searching for a weapon. A means of getting help. *Anything.* There was the lamp, but it was too heavy for her one hand to lift. And the telephone would be too heavy. That left only the little milk-glass vase of daisies.

Summoning all her will, she stretched her arm out along the tabletop, trying to reach the red telephone button that meant room service. Slowly, too slowly, she thought, her fingers crept along the varnished wood, trying to reach—

Kevin had a knife in his hand, one of the carving knives used by the waiters to slice the lamb at dinner. It was wide and long and honed.

She lunged for the telephone, felt the button give under the pressure of stiffened fingers. She tried to knock off the receiver. Failed. Her hand flailed, fingers stretched in desperation. Again she reached the room service button, but her fingers fell away. Falling back, her hand found the base of the little flower vase. She clawed to hold it, pull it—

Kevin lifted the blade to strike.

TWENTY-FIVE

12:10 a.m., Friday, May 13

ROMEO POPOI, finished with the evening's work, relaxed on a stool in the room service office. The Hepplewhite maintained what it called a "selective" all-night room service menu: cold sandwiches and salad plates with cold nonalcoholic drinks. It was rarely used. Hungry, late-night clientele were encouraged to visit the Gardenia Room or the Day Lily. After midnight no coffee, or hot soup or spirits were delivered. Breakfast service began at 6:00 a.m., dinner service stopped at nine, supper at eleven. So room service, between midnight and six, was called the "graveyard," and the unfortunates who worked it were apprentice housemen, beginning bellmen and junior kitchen help. And even then they were only asked to "pull the graveyard" once every two weeks as extra duty for extra pay. Normally two people were assigned.

Tonight Romeo Popoi had taken one place. He usually slept in Mr. V's office until it was his turn to deliver something, and then he dozed again. But tonight Romeo wasn't sleepy. He sat on the stool and pondered ways to clear his father's name. Mr. V had promised to help him.

He saw the light flash on the service switchboard for room 444. "Kitchen," he answered, the way he'd been taught. But no one answered; obviously the person hadn't yet picked up the telephone receiver. That happened sometimes, he'd been told. Just wait a little. Then if the person doesn't connect with you, ignore the summons.

Romeo waited, his mind on his father. "Hello," he said finally, "this is the kitchen, room service. How may we help?"

There was still no response.

"All right," he said into the mouthpiece, "no tuna fish sandwich for you."

He hung up and went back to the diagram of the Hepplewhite record room that Mr. V had given him. Tomorrow, in his free time, he meant to start on filing cabinet E, where the list of suppliers for old Hepplewhite parties was housed. Mr. V had suggested that as a place to start to find evidence of kickbacks in Romeo's father's day.

"But I must tell you, Romeo," Eduardo Vinici had said, "that there are ways hotels have operated from the times of the Caesars, and the kickback is how business is done and proper delivery assured. I, myself, couldn't succeed without it."

Room 444 flashed again, a short weak flare. But Romeo's head was bent over his diagram and his thoughts were far away. He missed it.

The flash wasn't repeated.

THE VASE CLUNG to Cecilia's damp palm. Despairingly, she swung her arm and crashed it over Kevin's head. It shattered against his skull, and scented water drenched his face and ran into his eyes. Aging daisies dangled in his hair. Dazed, he plunged the knife. The blade flew down, grazed Cecilia's left breast and pierced through the quilt and sheets to the mattress. A long thread of red bubbled in her side. Somehow she was screaming, her strength was returning, and someone was pounding at her door.

Eduardo Vinici, master key in his hand, turned the lock of the door. He and Detective Tyrone Scott barged into the room.

Cecilia, half-naked, splattered with blood, held the jagged-edged vase tightly against Kevin Wilder's throat. The long knife stayed, hilt high, in the bed. Kevin was afraid to move. Cecilia leaned returning strength upon the broken glass and wondered how Mr. V and Scotty had known to come. It took great effort to keep her eyes open.

"Women," Mr. V said admiringly. "They sure aren't what they used to be."

"Agreed," Tyrone Scott said. "Damn good effort on your part, Cecilia." He took the broken vase from her trembling hand. "Move and I'll cut you myself," he said to Kevin. He hauled Kevin off the bed and shoved him into the chair. "Call the precinct," he ordered Mr. V.

"Oh, delighted," Mr. V responded.

Cecilia, covering herself, pointed to her open hand-bag. "He told me," she gasped thinly, but her voice was coming back. "And my tape recorder's in there, on top. It's voice-activated, so maybe..."

"Honey, you're my kind of girl," Tyrone Scott said.

TWENTY-SIX

12:00 p.m., Friday

IT'S INTERESTING—now that it's over—how Scotty
determined it was Kevin. Well, really, he didn't. It was
Mr. Vinici who showed Scotty the way and really
cracked the case. Then Detective Scott solved it. Or
maybe I did. I had the tape recorder, after all.

Remember, diary, when I mentioned Scotty's talk
the first night? He said it was important to remember
the things that happened before a crime took place.
Well, that was it. Simplicity itself, and the biggest,
dumbest mistake ever, the kind you wouldn't think to
plot because it's too human.

Here's what happened—Mr. V recognized Kevin
from his and Muriel's "Wednesday matinees." It took
him a while to mention it to Detective Scott, he was so
preoccupied with his own troubles. But finally he remembered "Madame Lake's luncheon visitor," as
Kevin was referred to by the hotel staff. He always
came around twelve-thirty and went straight up to her
suite, where they always ordered the same meal. Kevin
never left the room once he went up, except to leave
the premises, which he generally did about four. It was
standing hotel gossip, the mystery writer and her baby-
boy lover. Muriel would come in to plan things with

Mr. Vinici, stay the day in the Franklin Delano Roosevelt Suite, and sometimes the night. When she spent the night, Augustus Graves was the roommate, in for dinner. She had a standing reservation for the Franklin Delano Roosevelt Suite every Wednesday until the conference was over.

But here's the fascinating thing. I'm sure Kevin is aware of his charm and he's quite self-confident, but he never stopped to think that in this big hotel he would be remembered. He never watched *Upstairs/Downstairs* on television, I guess, because if he had, he would have known full well: servants and hotel personnel know *everything*.

Well, once Mr. V came to Detective Scott with that information, Scotty watched Kevin closely. And then, last night, after the fingerprinting and before dinner, Kevin asked Scotty if he was ready to make an arrest. So Scotty told him yes, Augustus Graves would be charged after a case could be assembled. And after the movie, once Detective Scott thought everyone should have had time to get back to their rooms and settle down, he had gone up to have a talk with Kevin. Only Kevin wasn't in his room; he was in mine. So Detective Scott waited over an hour, pacing the hall around the corner, until almost midnight, and then he called Mr. V, who is discretion itself, and asked to be let into Kevin's room with the master key. Mr. V obliged him, but they found nothing incriminating. Then the clock downstairs struck twelve. They could barely hear it from Kevin's room, but it reminded Scotty that Kevin had gone upstairs with me. So he decided to run Kevin down in my room. If we were dressed, Detective Scott said, he meant to ask Kevin to come out and talk. Mr. V tagged along; just curiosity, he said.

And that's how Detective Scott and Mr. V arrived at my door. When I didn't answer, Scotty asked Mr. V to use his key. The detective was very humble about the rescue. He said I'd been doing all right on my own and hadn't needed his help. Though, of course, I did, diary.

I went to Lenox Hill Hospital for emergency stitches; they gave me seventeen and took blood samples to determine what Kevin had slipped into my drink. It turned out to be medication from DDT's kit. The doctor, Jane Bowman was her name, said the stitches were necessary to reduce my scarring and that my left breast and side would be tender for a while, even after the stitches come out in ten days.

While I was at the hospital, Herman Patrick was awakened and asked to look for Kevin's telephone number, which was, plain as mustaches, the number I'd found in Muriel's dress. So Kevin never would have, could have, gotten away with murder. And his novel won't be published, either, now that the real *Unforgivable Sin* has been found.

By six this morning, oh, diary, the papers had the news and made such a fuss. Suddenly I was the third woman mystery writer selected to be murdered by "the plagiarist," as they called Kevin. My publicity photo and headline ran the whole first page of the tabloids. There was a small written piece, under the fold, on the first page of the *New York Times*. My minute interview in the ballroom with Mr. Graves at my side was run on TV several times. I was dubbed ''The Third Time's Charm.'' Oh, it really was fun and exciting. My telephone rang off the hook, even though the management downstairs had been told to hold my calls, and Mr. Enders, Hepplewhite's general manager, changed my room. I thought about asking for the Franklin Delano Roosevelt Suite, but I didn't. Still, maybe next time? Mr. Graves sent me a stupendous bouquet of flowers, and he told me my new book, re-named *Slumber Said the Sandman*, is already in auction. I'll be a rich author before *Death Wakes Up*, the original title, ever sees a bookstore. Golly.

I must confess that all the hullabaloo has made me exceedingly happy. Success is great. Alice Ludlow is going to be my editor, now that Haunting House and Tombstone have merged into GravesGate Books, and my novel will be their first lead title. Incredible. All the talk shows want to book me, and an agent's been calling from Hollywood about adapting *Slumber* for the movies. Mr. Graves says he'll handle that, and what I should do is get out of the Hepplewhite and start on my next book.

I say yes to that.

Tonight, lucky Friday the thirteenth, I stood at the podium in Ballroom B in front of, it seemed, hundreds of people. Because of the publicity the Hepplewhite had to tear down the library and set in additional dinner tables. I was really addressing two ballrooms—me who used to stutter in writing class.

It was strange standing up there in front of all those writers of whom, just days ago, I had been so in awe. Too quickly I had become one of them. I stood there in Muriel's beautiful gown which, because my side had to be thickly wrapped, was too tight in the bodice and therefore showed my bosom. Alice Ludlow criticized me for that after, but Gordon Gates, Augustus Graves and even Jonathan Pells all told me I wore the dress well. In fact, Stash Yarrow actually asked me out! But the thrill of Mr. Yarrow has gone for me and I said no thank you. I danced with Detective Scott at the party afterward.

Well, I stood up there reading Muriel Lake's notes as I'd planned, and I was aware that some of the eyes out there weren't friendly. Some of the writers were content to be themselves and to struggle on at their trade and take the breaks as they came, good and bad. Those looked at me with welcome and no malice. But others resented my good fortune, and I saw in their eyes the same kind of motivation that must have taken hold of Kevin. I thought, as I stood up there, in the background of the award-winning writers' speeches, that I wouldn't go to Hollywood or to some exotic place to write my next book. I would stay home like anybody else. I pledged that I would lead a simple life, attend to my work, respect the achievements of others and not be corrupted by the privileges of success.

And I would begin, I promised, by writing a full report of this conference as I had been asked to do.

When it came my turn at the end for closing remarks, I thanked everyone in Muriel Lake's name and

DDT's and my own. We all owe a debt to one another, I said. We're all running together on the same two-way street. We owe the writers long before us and the colleagues we will never know who will come after. And they owe us.

Then I stood down. Scotty was waiting for me.

This, then, is my report of the Writers of Mystery's New York Conference. It was compiled with the help of everyone concerned, even the villain's, and it is as truthful as I can make it.

I learned many things from that week at the Hepplewhite. Wisdom won must be remembered or be lost. What is right doesn't change. But people change, as do circumstances and points of view. There's the danger. Success or failure can either corrupt or inspire. What's right and decent in a human soul stays the course only if it gets enough attention and daily care and, from time to time, a proper shine.

Respectfully submitted,

Cecilia Burnett, Recording Secretary, WOM

PS: At midnight on Friday, in our own little ceremony, Scotty, Mr. V and I met to turn off the chimes on that grandfather clock. Mr. V, compliments of the Hepplewhite, poured us champagne.

> "Nothing is more satisfying than a mystery concocted by one of the pros."
> —*L.A. Times*

Hugh Pentecost
Winner of the Mystery Writers of America Award

TIME OF TERROR $3.50 ☐
The elegant calm of New York's plush Hotel Beaumont is shattered when a heavily-armed madman plants bombs in the building and holds two guests hostage. Manager Pierre Chambrun's only chance is to outwit the ruthless killer at his own game.

BARGAIN WITH DEATH $3.50 ☐
Pierre Chambrun, legendary manager of Hotel Beaumont has only hours to find the answers to some lethal questions when a ruthless killer turns the hotel into a deathtrap.

REMEMBER TO KILL ME $3.50 ☐
Pierre Chambrun must cope with the shooting of a close friend, a hostage situation and a gang of hoods terrorizing guests.

NIGHTMARE TIME $3.50 ☐
After the disappearance of an Air Force major involved in the Star Wars program, Chambrun must use some extraordinary measures to decide whether the disappearance is an act of treason or the hotel is harboring a killer with diplomatic immunity.

Total Amount	$	_____
Plus 75¢ Postage		.75
Payment Enclosed	$	_____

To order please send your name, address and zip or postal code with a check or money order payable to Worldwide Library Mysteries to:

In the U.S.
Worldwide Library Mysteries
901 Fuhrmann Blvd.
Box 1325
Buffalo, NY   14269-1325

In Canada
Worldwide Library Mysteries
P.O. Box 609
Fort Erie, Ontario
L2A 5X3

Please specify book title with your order.

MYS-12

WORLDWIDE LIBRARY®

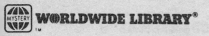

Order now the spine-tingling mysteries you missed in stores.

THE HABIT OF FEAR—Dorothy Salisbury Davis $3.50 ☐
New York columnist Julie Hayes struggles to regain her equilibrium
by traveling to Ireland in search of her father after a seemingly
random act of violence shatters her life. Her pursuit leads her into a
maze of violence, mystery—and murder.

THERE HANGS THE KNIFE—Marcia Muller $3.50 ☐
Joanna Stark's scheme to entrap one of the world's greatest art thieves
has gone murderously awry. Plunging deep into Britain's fabulous art
world and terrifying underworld, she must confront her nightmarish
past as she races to recover two valuable stolen paintings ... and stay
alive in the bargain.

KIRBY'S LAST CIRCUS—Ross H. Spencer $3.50 ☐
Small-time private eye Birch Kirby has been noticed by the CIA.
They like his style. Nobody can be that inept, they believe, and they
need somebody with imagination to save the world from ultimate
catastrophe. As he goes undercover as the bull-pen catcher of the No
Sox baseball team, Kirby keeps an eye on the KGB, whose secret
messages cannot be decoded.

Total Amount	$ _____
Plus 75¢ Postage	.75
Payment Enclosed	$ _____

To order please send your name, address and zip or postal code with a check or money order
payable to Worldwide Library Mysteries to:

In the U.S.
Worldwide Library Mysteries
901 Fuhrmann Blvd.
Box 1325
Buffalo, NY 14269-1325

In Canada
Worldwide Library Mysteries
P.O. Box 609
Fort Erie, Ontario
L2A 5X3

Please specify book title with your order.

MYS-14

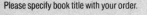

W⊕RLDWIDE LIBRARY®

Don't miss these Worldwide Mysteries from award-winning authors!

MURDER MOST STRANGE—Dell Shannon $3.50 ☐
Spring fever has hit Lieutenant Luis Mendoza both on the job and at
home. But it hasn't eased the LAPD's endless caseload of bizarre
crimes and difficult cases "Dapper Dan" the rapist and murderer ... a
stick-up artist who has found a foolproof weapon ... a gruesome
double homicide/suicide with a weird twist ... all add up to months of
Murder Most Strange, and Mendoza knows it's time to finally clean
house.

A QUESTION OF MURDER—Eric Wright $3.50 ☐
Police inspector Charlie Salter is assigned to safeguard Toronto's
fashionable Yorkville section while the British princess is visiting. He
tries to control what looks like a feud between the business owners
and the street merchants when a bomb goes off, killing one of the
shopkeepers.

BOOKED FOR DEATH—Miriam Borgenicht $3.50 ☐
Shortly after Celia Sommerville told her fiancé, George, that she
wouldn't marry him, his body turned up in a sleepy Vermont town.
Dead of a broken heart—and a self-inflicted gunshot wound. Celia is
determined to prove that cautious, pedantic George would not take his
own life. Her investigation reveals that a lot of people have reason to
want him dead. But who pulled the trigger?

Total Amount	$ _____
Plus 75¢ Postage	.75
Payment Enclosed	$ _____

To order please send your name, address and zip or postal code with a check or money order
payable to Worldwide Library Mysteries to:

In the U.S.
Worldwide Library Mysteries
901 Fuhrmann Blvd.
Box 1325
Buffalo, NY 14269-1325

In Canada
Worldwide Library Mysteries
P.O. Box 609
Fort Erie, Ontario
L2A 5X3

Please specify book title with your order.   MYS-15

W⊕RLDWIDE LIBRARY®